FOR MELODY'S CHILD

Kayla C McIntyre

First published in 2019 by Kayla C. McIntyre

www.kaylacmcintyre.com

All rights reserved

Copyright © Kayla C. McIntyre 2019

Text and Illustrations Copyright © Kayla C. McIntyre 2019

Copyright with UKCCS Reg. No. 284726368

The digital edition was published in 2019.

The right of Kayla C. McIntyre to be identified as the author of this work has been asserted by her.

This book is sold subject to the condition that it shall not, by way of trade or otherwise, be lent, hired out or otherwise circulated in any form of binding or cover other than that in which it is published. No part of this publication may be reproduced, stored in a retrieval system or transmitted in any form or by any means (electronic, mechanical, photocopying, recording or otherwise) without prior written permission from Kayla C McIntyre. Requests are to be sent to:

Kaylacmcintyre@gmail.com

This is a fictitious story and is not intended to reflect any one person's life. Names, characters, places, incidents and dialogues are products of the author's imagination or are used fictitiously. Any resemblance to actual people, living or dead, events or locales is entirely coincidental. This story is not about any particular IVF clinic and does not reflect all IVF clinical policies.

This novel has been written in British English.

ISBN 9781513646824

Cover Art by Cheriefox.com

Edited by RB Writing Services

Professional Proofreading Services by Sarah Jessah

A NOTE FROM THE AUTHOR

I am a single mother who has lived her own amazing journey to have her precious child. I have felt a yearning, for a long time now, to write a story to inspire and empower as many other women as I can.

Giving life to a child has been a momentous event for me, and every day I feel the joy, love, companionship and contentment this child has brought into my life.

I am so thankful I walked along this pathway.

WRITTEN FOR

All the single women out there who desperately wish to have their own child.

'THERE IS HOPE'

THANK YOU

My precious, amazing, unique and beautiful child – for just being 'you'.

Anne, Eva and Emily – For all your opinions, thoughts, suggestions and constructive feedback. These were priceless.

Jo – For your encouragement, handwritten notes, telling me to 'have faith in myself' and this quote...

**'She Believed She Could
So She Did'**

To all my other fabulous friends who gave me bits and pieces of advice along the way.

Chapter One

****

Melody was full of anticipation as she entered the dance hall. She'd been looking forward to tango classes for weeks now, and she was excited to have finally got a place.

She scanned the rapidly filling room and was surprised by the variety of participants. There were middle-aged couples learning together, misfit sweaty gentlemen, single, intelligent-looking older ladies and men who appeared to be divorcees. There were also several young university students, and one mysterious, solo young man.

After a couple of minutes, the dance instructor, Lucas, told everyone to get into three lines. He directed the ladies to stand to the left and the men to stand to the right. Lucas took charge of directing the men's dance steps, whilst his curvy, long-legged dance partner – Sofia – took the ladies through theirs. Melody observed and followed Sofia's and Lucas' sleek dance steps eagerly, as did everybody else in the room.

Although Lucas slowed his moves down, the room full of beginners were obviously lacking in fluency. Melody chuckled to herself at how hilarious the sight would be to any observers. She privately admired Lucas' looks; he had a sultry, Latino vibe about him. He was tall and athletic, and his eyes were dark and intense. Every woman in the dance school secretly lusted after him.

Halfway through the class, Lucas and Sofia demonstrated the tango. It was after that that they finally instructed everyone to pair up. One dance, then everyone changed partners. Another dance and they changed again, and so on and so forth. Melody was thrilled when she got to dance with the mysterious young man she'd spotted upon her entrance. Like Lucas, this man was fit and muscular, clearly talented and confident. His hair was a sun-bleached blond, which was stylishly cut and he was tall with broad shoulders. His green eyes were simply striking against his tanned complexion. It was immediately obvious that he'd been to tango classes previously. He had fluidity in his steps, and real assuredness oozed through his dance moves. He seemed to effortlessly move his body in time to the music, and Melody thought he could have been an instructor himself. Melody enjoyed dancing with him immensely, and he smiled at her and looked boldly into her eyes throughout their first dance. He expertly led her into each tango position effortlessly and smoothly corrected her when she misplaced her feet. On their third dance together, they introduced themselves to each other. The young man's name was Dexter.

Melody herself had a natural flair for dancing. In her youth, she'd been talented at ballet and had learned the violin. She naturally felt musical rhythm and couldn't help but tap her feet to the Latin music, even as they stood still.

This shared musical talent could be one of the reasons Melody and Dexter naturally hit it off. After attending several sessions together, it wasn't long before their enthusiasm for tango became an excitement about seeing each other. It was obvious to everyone who observed, they were becoming more than just dance partners.

As varied a bunch as the dance class was, everyone soon became good friends. After two weeks in, most of them started to go after class for drinks at the tapas bar, located a few doors down from the dance hall.

It wasn't until about six weeks into the dance lessons that Dexter and Melody found themselves alone one night at a table.

"So, how are you enjoying the dance classes, Melody?" Dexter asked, sitting across the table from her and looking into her eyes, with the same boldness as he had during their first dance.

"I love them!" Melody replied, feeling slightly giddy to be in Dexter's presence. "I feel alive when I dance. I'm enjoying the Latin music too."

"Yeah. It's great, isn't it?" said Dexter.

Dexter looked intensely into Melody's eyes. "I love the way you dance," he said.

Melody blushed a little, and she was glad to be in the dark surroundings of the tapas bar. "Thank you," she said, feeling her heart racing. "I love dancing with you."

Dexter looked into Melody's eyes again and gently asked her, "Do you live by yourself?"

Melody met Dexter's intense gaze and replied, "Well, yes, I do."

The tension in the air was electric and she thought she would test some waters. "Something tells me that you share with a bunch of lads. I bet it's a house full of chaos." She smiled as she said it and gave him a teasing wink.

He laughed, still staring into her eyes and smiling. "You've got me there. I do!" He took a deep breath, "Something tells me, you have a snugly double bed."

Melody smiled. "I sure do. Queen size, in fact. Very comfy and a bit creaky!" Her voice broke as she said it, and their eyes locked as their minds both wandered. Their energy was scorching. Melody glanced down at Dexter's clothing.

Dexter was wearing a very hip blue and green striped dress shirt. He was always well-dressed, and when he raised his arm to twirl Melody, she often caught a glimpse of his Hugo Boss underwear.

Melody was shorter than Dexter, and her figure was voluptuous. She loved to wear a headband to keep her brunette hair away from her face, and this gave her a slightly hippy look. Her favourite possession was her sky-blue Vespa scooter. Scootie, she called him. She'd decided her scooter was of the male variety.

Although they looked quite different, the pair

immediately looked just like that: a pair. As they chatted in the tapas bar that evening, long after their fellow dance class friends had left, they discovered that they both lived on the outskirts of the city of Auckland. They arranged that night that Dexter would take Melody to the tango dance party at Viaduct Harbour the following Saturday.

They were both, on some level, aware that it would be the start of something special.

Chapter Two

****

Melody dressed casually for the dance party, blue jeans and her favourite black hippy-style top. This was her favourite 'going out' top. It had a low V-neck and flared out between the elbows and wrists. A hint of her cleavage showed through the top, but she was happy about that. She'd never appreciated her full figure as a young girl, but more and more she had grown to feel more comfortable within her own skin. Her freshly blow-dried brunette hair was smooth and shiny, and flowed softly past her shoulders. To keep her hair off her face, she wore a light pink headband with a printed black and green flowery design on it. Melody wore just a little blusher and eye makeup and smiled at herself in the mirror. She placed her favourite dress ring, which had a ruby as the centre piece, on her right middle finger. She was ready.

Perched on her bed as she waited, Melody was full

of high hopes. She heard a car and jumped up to look out of the window. Her heart pounded as she saw it was the car and driver she'd been waiting for. Dexter drove a black sports car, and the engine purred just loudly enough to be heard from indoors. Melody grabbed her black handbag and walked downstairs as she heard his knock on the door. She opened it and immediately inhaled his scent.

Dexter smelt of spicy aftershave, which Melody enjoyed breathing in deeply as she took in his outfit.

"Hey," she said. "We match!"

Sure enough, he wore an outfit similar to hers. His shirt was long-sleeved and black, whilst he wore jeans on his lower half. Melody admired how he looked in the outfit, reflecting on how the black shirt complemented his tanned skin. His blond hair looked ruffled and messy, but the style suited him.

"Hello," he said, grinning at Melody. "Have you been checking out my wardrobe?"

Dexter turned to look at his car. "Shall we go?" He asked Melody, pointing his key and pushing a button to unlock the door.

"Yes, let's go," Melody replied with a smile. "We have a party to go to!"

She lifted her handbag over her shoulder, closed and locked the front door, then walked with Dexter to his car.

"I love your car! I thought you might drive something like this," she said, smiling and feeling embarrassed as she walked towards the passenger door.

Dexter walked ahead and opened the door for her. "I'm glad you approve," he replied, in a mock-posh voice. He nodded his head to gesture for Melody to step inside.

"Thank you," said Melody, still smiling as she slid into the front seat.

Dexter gently closed the door.

How nice, she thought. *What a gentlemanly gesture.* She liked him even more.

Their trip to Viaduct Harbour was a trip full of good humour, jokes and singing to a myriad of songs they knew together. Melody looked at Dexter and felt an odd sensation she'd been here before. Looking at his profile, she felt déjà vu and the sense there would be many more fun times like this.

The trip to the dance party was over too quickly when they arrived at the nightclub. It was set in a beautiful location on the edge of the harbour. The water lapped up to the base of the building, and the balcony appeared to hover just above the water level. Dancers were able to enjoy the splendid views of the lights reflecting on the water as they danced. They linked arms as they walked towards the entrance together, and Dexter pulled the tickets from his jeans pocket. He flashed a smile at the bulky man on the door and held the tickets up. The door man silently nodded and pointed the pair in. Dexter gently placed his arm on Melody's waist as they walked into the buzzing room together. The dance club was filled with people: far more than were commonly seen in their dance classes. Outfits varied from jeans and tops – similar to their own – all the way to sexy cocktail attire. Dexter and Melody immediately danced together, glowing as they moved to the hypnotic Latin beat and enjoying the passionate closeness of the tango.

Throughout the evening, they danced with many partners from their dance school, but they were constantly drawn back to each other. It was impossible to ignore the magnetic pull they shared as they dazzled together. Everybody noticed. It was hard not to. Some eyebrows were raised by friends as they departed at the end of the night, leaving the pair laughing as they half walked, half skipped to the car together.

It was during the trip back that their chemistry heightened even more. When Dexter stopped the car outside Melody's home, they both turned to face each other. After gazing into each other's eyes for several seconds, Melody and Dexter's lips locked in a passionate and enduring kiss. Their warm mouths danced together as though the music was still playing and Melody lost her breath completely as the kiss overwhelmed her senses.

Reluctantly, she pulled away. "Thank you so much for an amazing night," she said, feeling dizzy and faint.

"Thank you, Melody. You are definitely my favourite dance partner," Dexter replied as he took a deep breath.

Melody smiled and felt disorientated as she picked up her bag. "Goodbye," she said softly, as Dexter remained in the driver's seat.

"See you soon, Melody," he said.

Chapter Three

****

Dexter watched Melody open her front door and step into her home.

Wow, he thought. *What an incredible night!*

Dexter loved spending time with Melody. As he drove to the home he shared with three other rowdy young men, he was lost in thoughts of her. He thought about her smile and the way her eyes sparkled when she looked at him. When they held hands, he was conscious of how she made his heart flutter. Dexter loved Melody's body. He loved her curves. She was so womanly. The way she moved her body as well... *Wow*, he thought again.

He slowed his car down and parked on the road. *He really must find some new flatmates soon*, he thought as he tried to open the car door. The recycle bin, which was piled high with empty beer bottles, was teetering close to his car. Dexter squeezed out of the door and moved the bin further along the footpath to a more stable position.

When he came back to collect his wallet from the car and just before closing the car door, he saw the silver sparkle of Melody's ruby ring out of the corner of his eye.

He bent down to pick it up, and smiled as he held it close to him.

Chapter Four

****

Melody awoke with a long, slow stretch and a smile on her face. All her memories from the previous night came wafting back to her.

Aaaaahhhhh.... What a blissful night, she thought.

Melody was a student studying Beauty Therapy, concentrating more on natural and holistic therapies. It was her passion. Natural therapies were becoming more and more popular in New Zealand, and even more so in Auckland, where she lived. She shone as a student, and she especially loved the ability to sleep in during her late starts. Previous to this, she'd been a travel agent, but had made the decision to change her career. Melody had grown up with her parents on their farm and, although she missed the views of the wheat growing on the paddocks, she adored living in the city. It was the city that made her buzz, that filled her with life.

Dexter was working as a Marketing Consultant. A sleep-in was not possible, so the day after the party was difficult for him. His priorities in life at present were having fun and he had taken this job merely due to knowing a friend who already worked there. Plus, there were also a number of attractive girls who worked in the company.

His life was quite different to hers, but she was excited and energized by him, as he was her.

Melody picked up her phone from the bedside table and texted.

'Good morning sexy, yawn, stretch... Aaahhh, the pros of being a student!'

'Good morning gorgeous. Hey, you left your ring in my car last night.'

'Oh! Did I? I didn't even realise!'

'I guess we should have lunch together, so I can return it. LOL! Are you sure you didn't leave it in my car on purpose?'

'No, but I'm glad I did!'

'Can you drag yourself out of bed and meet me at The Trendy Kiwi cafe in the City at 1pm?'

'I'll try. ;) See you then!'

Melody stretched and yawned again. It was her day off from class today. She hauled herself out of bed and had a quick breakfast and a long shower. What a perfect day it was today. She lived in a beautiful city, and she didn't have to travel far from Auckland to see magical and spellbinding scenery. She felt lucky to be alive. After dressing in colourful clothes and straightening her hair, she applied a touch of make-up. Melody was ready. She pulled her beloved Scootie out of the garage, and off she rode to The Trendy Kiwi, home to the best iced chocolates in Auckland.

The Trendy Kiwi was a quaint little cafe, and it was like walking into a cave. But the darkness inside was cool and welcoming, and was offset with subdued lighting. There was an outdoor area behind the cafe, which was in contrast to the inside, as it was light, bright and airy. They met outside the cafe on the footpath.

"Hi," said Melody. "Ahh! What a sleep!"

"Jealous!" said Dexter. "I think I've nearly fallen asleep on my computer at least twice today! I'm going to squash my nose." He laughed, touching his nose.

"Oh, don't do that! I love that nose," Melody said,

reaching out to stroke the sleeve of his green shirt.

They walked into the cafe and were welcomed by the friendly staff behind the counter. There were couples snuggled up on the comfortable large sofas in the cafe and groups of friends were playing chess and draughts at the tables inside. Melody and Dexter walked through the cafe and found a shady table outside. Dexter promptly gave Melody her precious ring and smiled widely at her.

"Thank you!" said Melody. "I would have been searching everywhere for this."

"You're welcome," Dexter replied still smiling.

A waitress walked over and they both ordered bacon and camembert cheese Panini and fries with a cappuccino.

"Last night was fantastic," said Dexter, looking at Melody across the table.

"It was," Melody said. "I loved dancing there with you and the venue was amazing!"

"It was all mind-blowing," said Dexter, pointing at Melody's green cotton top.

"Hey! We match again!" he said, laughing.

"Oh my!" said Melody. She hadn't noticed, having got dressed in a bit of a daze herself.

The waitress came out with their food and drinks on a tray. They ate slowly, as they were both hyped and nervous.

"You know, I have no idea what you do," said Melody as she put a fry in her mouth.

"Well, I work in Marketing, making up slogans and things like that, just down the road," replied Dexter.

"Do you like it?" Melody asked.

"Yeah, it's all right. My boss can be pretty demanding, but it's okay. Sometimes I think I should have been a computer geek though. Everyone is always asking me to fix their computer at work!"

"Oh, don't mention computers... I bought a new computer last week and it took me ages to set it up. My ex took my old computer when he moved out and I'm still getting sorted after leaving that house. It's taking me ages! I still haven't hung up my pictures on the wall!" Melody said, screwing up her face.

"I can help you with that, if you like," offered Dexter.

"Really? Oh wow, that would be amazing!" Melody said. "I've missed having my photos and pictures on the wall."

They talked some more until it was time for Dexter to return to work. Both of them looked at their lunch, which had only been half eaten. The air was simply too exhilarating to eat. They both had their meals transferred to takeaway containers and took them with them. Outside the cafe, they gave each other a nervous hug. Their lips softly met as they intoxicated each other with their energy for several seconds.

Energy that was so dazzling, it was blinding.

Chapter Five

****

It was a glorious Saturday morning. The sun was shining, and not a cloud was in the sky. There was just a soft breath of air blowing. Melody was finishing her breakfast of pancakes when she heard a text arrive on her phone.

'Hi sexy, how are you?'

'Great, gorgeous man. Splendid day today!'

'It is a splendid handyman day! Are you home this morning? I've dug out my tools and I can help you hang up your pictures.'

'Yes! I sure am. Come on over!'

Forty-five minutes later, Melody could hear the familiar hum of Dexter's car approaching and felt that familiar flutter of excitement in her belly.

She opened her front door before he knocked, and stood smiling at Dexter as he approached carrying his tool box.

"Hi," she said as he walked towards her.

"Hi," replied Dexter, squeezing through the door, angling his tool box so it didn't scratch the paintwork.

They kissed tenderly and hugged affectionately.

"You have a lot of pictures!" he remarked. Dexter looked around him and all along the walls and weaving up the steps to the first floor, were intermittent pictures delicately leaning on the walls.

"I love all of them! I've placed them in the spots where I'm hoping to hang them. They've been like this for weeks now," replied Melody. "Thank you so much for helping, Dexter."

They worked together to securely hang the pictures. Dexter using his drill and Melody giving subtle instructions. "A little to the left, oh, no, just a tad bit to the right."

When all the pictures were perfectly aligned downstairs and on the stairwell, they went into Melody's bedroom. Her bedroom balcony doors were wide open, allowing a pleasant breeze into the room.

Melody lived in a small two-bedroom house, and it

was the perfect size for her. Her favourite place in the house was her cute bedroom balcony and she would often sit there reading a book. There was always a symphony of different birds chirping and singing in the trees not far away. The Rosellas were especially loud at this time of year. There was one Kingfisher who took a liking to Melody and would often sit on the balcony railing close to her. He would swoop down to the ground when he spied some moving lunch and would return to the balcony again.

Dexter's biceps bulged as he carried his tool box into her room, then he put it on the floor. "We're having a hot summer," he said as he took off his t-shirt.

He leant over the box, searching for some more screws. His upper torso was a clear olive complexion, with not a spot on it, and he had a six-pack! Melody stared at him, speechless and stunned! He had a beautiful body. Dexter proceeded to drill a hole at the spot marked with an X. Melody could see droplets of perspiration on the middle of his back, and she imagined licking them off. *Oh dear*, she thought to herself. *Get hold of yourself, girl.*

Dexter turned around to get a different kind of

screw from his tool box. Melody was mesmerised as she stared at his body while he worked. There was a small amount of hair on his chest and his pecs were perfect. She almost salivated as she admired his body.

Dexter stepped back from hanging the last of the pictures and picked up his t-shirt. He pulled it back on, then said to Melody, "What a difference a few pictures makes. Your place looks so homely now."

"Thank you. You've done a wonderful job! It is perfect!" Melody replied.

Both are perfect, she thought.

Chapter Six

****

Dexter collected Melody at her home again on yet another outing to the dance party at Viaduct Harbour. It was fast becoming their favourite place to go together.

On the way, Dexter gave Melody a CD which he compiled himself for her. It was a combination of the latest dance hits which they both loved. They listened to the CD in the car and enjoyed singing along. Melody did tend to get the words wrong, but that made the experience all the more special. Dexter constantly teased her for messing up the lyrics, but he secretly loved this little quirk of hers. It was endearing and funny.

When they arrived at the Latin dance club, they passionately kissed in the car park. They would have been happy to stay in the car together all night. Eventually, they made their way to the tango dance party, where they once again danced the night away, dancing with other partners as well, but always coming back to each other. They were both getting closer and closer and falling for each other.

After the dance party, they decided to move on to another bar on the Harbour. They walked hand in hand, taking in the breathtaking views of the Harbour as they walked. The lights from the surrounding bars and fine dining restaurants illuminated the water in a soft hue, creating a spellbinding ambiance. The luxurious yachts gently bobbed up and down on the water, and the rippling waves swished up against the harbour wall. The night air was filled with sounds of serenity from the water, and on the other side of them, the sounds of the Auckland nightlife. It was a delightful contrast for their senses. They didn't have to walk far before finding a perfect night spot. Viaduct Harbour was always buzzing and filled with excitement, and they quickly found a dance club they liked the look of. The club wasn't extremely busy, as it was a weeknight, so the dance floor wasn't overcrowded. The DJ played the latest dance hits, and many of the songs were the same songs Melody and Dexter had sung together on the way to the Harbour. They sexily danced, enjoying the rhythm of the music in the nightclub.

Before they knew it, it was 2 am in the morning. They finally dragged themselves away from the nightclub and walked along the pathway overlooking the Harbour on the way back to Dexter's car. Melody suddenly thought of a question she'd never thought to ask Dexter before.

"Dexter, can I ask how old you are?" Melody queried.

"Sure, I'm 24 years old," Dexter replied.

Melody gasped, "Really?" she said. She'd thought he was several years older than that.

"How old are you?" Dexter asked.

Melody paused for a second. "I'm 35," she said.

"You're kidding!" Dexter said. "I thought you were younger!"

Dexter and Melody were quite taken aback at this realisation, and they wondered what to make of this information. You would never guess their age difference, as they just looked perfect together and incredibly happy. An age difference of eleven years!

"Well," said Melody, 'I guess that makes you my toy boy!' She was trying to be light-hearted, but then she asked, "Does our age difference bother you?"

"No," said Dexter. "But I am surprised!"

They looked into each other's eyes before stepping into Dexter's car and both knew they didn't care how old they were. It felt right, they felt right. They simply felt perfect for each other.

Chapter Seven

****

Dexter turned off his computer and said goodnight to his work colleagues. After exiting the building, he crossed the road, dodging the traffic, and headed towards the car park to collect his car. Melody was on his mind again, and he pondered asking her out to dinner or the theatre. He would like the opportunity to get to know her better, away from the usual dance classes and dance parties.

As he thought it, something caught his eye. A poster. It was a windy afternoon, and the corner of the poster kept flipping up as the wind caught underneath it. It was like it was beckoning him. Dexter stopped to read it. The Lindy Hop Extravaganza Dance Show was playing at the theatre and he just knew Melody would love it. He looked at the dancers wearing 1940's style costumes on the poster. Dexter thought it sounded perfect and laughed out loud to himself, as he put the details in his phone.

That was sorted then; he would book the tickets as soon as he returned home. He was confident that Melody would say yes.

He couldn't wait to ask her.

Chapter Eight

****

As Melody was nearing the end of her studies, she'd managed to get a part-time job as a trainee Clinical Therapist in an anti-aging clinic. She advised mature and affluent clients on a system of facial peels, micro-dermabrasion, Botox, restaline and laser therapy treatments. She administered some treatments herself and also assisted the doctors with the more medical tasks. The best part was, she was able to look after herself and had access to excellent quality treatments and products. She enjoyed her new job immensely.

Melody was busy treating a patient's legs using the laser machine. She set the laser to vascular therapy, adjusted the wave length and frequency, and proceeded with the treatment. She quite liked treating unsightly veins on clients. It was quick, strangely therapeutic, and she saw results straight away. She did enjoy a good chat with her clients, also, and they easily opened up to her.

When she'd finished, she booked her client for a follow-up consultation and waved her goodbye.

This was the end of Melody's working day, so she picked up her phone. She discovered Dexter had sent her a text and she smiled as she read it.

'Hey sexy, I've got tickets to The Lindy Hop Extravaganza Dance Show at the theatre tonight. Would you like to go with me?'

'What? OMG!! I heard that show had sold out! How on Earth did you get them?'

'A friend owed me a favour. ;)'

'So impressed! I'd love to!'

'Great! I'll collect you at 6:30pm at yours.'

That night, Melody was putting the finishing touches to her makeup when she heard Dexter's car pulling up outside her house. She could feel his presence as he walked to her front door. He made her feel alive and full of energy. They both said hello, and kissed on the lips immediately.

Dexter escorted Melody out to his car and gentlemanly opened the car door for her. She beamed at him. They chatted, held hands and comfortably rested their hands on each other's legs intermittently as he drove. They arrived early for the show, so they went to a nearby bar to enjoy a drink together first. They sat at the bar, facing each other, as they both enjoyed their lemon, lime and vodka. There was no table between them, making the distance between them tiny and the tension enormous.

"Thank you so much for asking me to the show, Dexter. I'm really looking forward to it," said Melody, inching closer to where he sat.

"You're welcome," replied Dexter, with a sultry, sexy smile on his face. He was holding one of Melody's hands, caressing her fingers gently. He had perfectly manicured, soft hands for a man.

"I can't believe you got tickets to the show," said Melody.

"I waved my magical wand," replied Dexter with a cheeky grin. "We're in the second row too."

Melody burst out laughing. "No way!" she said. "Your friend must have owed you big time!"

"He did," Dexter said, still caressing her fingers. "He was stranded in the middle of nowhere, when his heap of rust car died. It was an eight-hour round trip to collect him! He works at the theatre and he managed to get hold of two tickets that are usually saved for VIP's."

"Well, I was hoping to see this show, but heard it had sold out. I'm feeling very lucky," said Melody with excitement.

"I have to admit," Dexter said, still caressing her fingers. "I couldn't imagine watching the show with anyone else."

Dexter looked at his watch. "We'd better go or we'll be late. Come on, sexy girl," he said. He stood up and held out his hand to escort Melody from the bar to the theatre.

As they walked, it started raining lightly. Dexter took off his jacket and held it over both their heads to shield them from the rain.

Just as the last call was announced, they arrived at the theatre. Melody and Dexter settled into their seats and watched the dance show hand in hand, their heads not far from one another. The show was brilliantly energetic and entertaining. The style and talent that each dancer displayed was enthralling and it was undeniably a dramatic, yet fun and cheeky performance. There was a romance story entwined within the performance and it was played out perfectly on stage. Melody and Dexter became absorbed and dazzled by the storyline, the dances, songs and music. Melody softly sung along to some of the songs, while Dexter intermittently watched her from the corner of his eye, smiling.

Afterwards, they arrived at Melody's home, and she invited Dexter inside. Melody led Dexter straight up to her bedroom. They fell onto the bed together and immediately entwined into a passionate kiss. Dexter removed Melody's dress and she unbuttoned his smart shirt. She stroked his chest as she climbed on top of him on the bed, whilst he kissed her breasts and neck. They were soon both naked, enjoying each other's bodies fully and without inhibitions. Although Dexter was younger than Melody, he was confident sexually and there was no nervousness as they made love. After a long, passionate lovemaking, they fell asleep together, before waking up in the morning to enjoy each other all over again.

It was late morning when they eventually got out of bed, both of them dazed and hungry. They walked to a cafe together, holding hands as they enjoyed the sunshine.

Sitting close together, Melody and Dexter relaxed during their lavish brunch. They looked into each other's eyes as they ate and enjoyed their newly developed connection.

Life felt amazing for both of them. They both longed for more passionate nights together.

Chapter Nine

****

The cafe was vibrant and full of chatter. Jazz music was playing in the background, and Dexter could make out the voice of Nora Jones singing.

The food was perfectly cooked, and Dexter enjoyed a big breakfast. It was big enough to fill the stomach of any Māori footballer. He looked across at Melody and watched her eat her scrambled eggs on toast. Just then, she looked up and their eyes met. She smiled at him, and even though she had a little scrambled egg on her lower lip, she made his heart melt. Dexter reached across and delicately removed the egg from her lip. He then put it on the edge of his plate and softly cupped her chin in his hand, all the while looking into her eyes.

He had never, ever felt like this before. Was there a cloud underneath his chair? He felt like he was hovering. Could this be the beginning of falling in love? Dexter didn't have much experience with women. He always made out he was experienced to his friends, to save face, but the truth was he'd done most of his research about women via the Internet and also by listening to his friends. He had never felt this connected to a woman before, and he was loving every single moment he spent with Melody.

He hoped this feeling would last forever.

Chapter Ten

****

Melody and Dexter were becoming a loving and caring couple. They both lived their separate and very different lives, but when they came together, they blended beautifully.

One day, Dexter was collecting Melody from work on Friday afternoon. Melody had finished her studies now and had been promoted to Clinical Therapist. She had been transferring her clients' 'before treatment' photos to their individual folders on the computer from the work camera. She wondered what she would find on the camera the following Monday morning. The thought made her laugh. Her boss and his wife were presidents of The Hardy Apples Nudist Club, and the previous Monday morning, she had found photos of her boss's wife naked on a boat with a group of other nudists. Thankfully, she'd not accidentally stumbled upon naked shots of her boss. The knowledge that he had been naked behind the camera was enough for her!

She'd just finished transferring the photos when Dexter arrived. He always looked so good, and his clothes were casually stylish. He wore a t-shirt with an urban art design and three-quarter cargo trousers with brand-name trainers on his feet. His sun-bleached blond hair was combed perfectly and his clear green eyes shone.

Melody left him waiting at reception whilst she changed out of her clinic uniform. She put on a long, flowing summer dress. The design was of blue and green flowers on a soft cream background, and it suited her colouring and full figure perfectly. She took her brunette hair out of her ponytail, and it cascaded over her shoulders. She swept it up on the sides only and fastened it with pretty clips to each side of her head, to hide the kink in her hair where her ponytail had been fastened. She put just a pinch of light pink blusher on her cheeks to give her complexion a glow. She was ready.

She met Dexter at the reception desk, said goodbye to her boss, and wished him a good weekend, trying not to giggle as she said it.

"How are you, gorgeous?" she asked Dexter, who was looking down at her. "I should have left my high heels on!"

"Great, especially better now." He smiled. "You look very cute. I like it when you have flat shoes on; you tuck nicely under my arm," said Dexter, winking at Melody. He put his arm around her.

"Thank you," replied Melody, snuggling into him. "You look handsome too. Hey, this is our first weekend away together. Oh, I'm so lucky to have such a great guy whisking me away for a romantic weekend."

"Where?" Dexter said, looking around.

"Very funny!" Melody said, "I'll keep this one!" She wrapped her arms around him and hugged him.

They walked together to Dexter's car hand in hand. Dexter drove Melody to scenic Red Beach, north of Auckland. He had booked a luxurious bed and breakfast accommodation overlooking the ocean. The drive only took thirty minutes, but they felt miles away from the busy city of Auckland. After they checked in, they made their way to the top floor. *What a sublime view!* They stood there on the balcony for a while, breathing in the fresh sea air, feeling hypnotised as the waves crashed into the shore then retracted back out to the sea again. The view was so awe-inspiring, Melody and Dexter stayed there for ages. They chatted and joked. They fed each other strawberries and entwined their arms romantically so they could sip from each other's champagne glasses.

"I'm so glad I met you, Melody," Dexter said. "We always have so much fun together," he added.

"Oh, I know. I don't think I've had a connection like this with another man before. I think we have something special together," she replied.

"I do too," he said.

They snuggled in closer together and fed each other strawberries again. "Does our age difference bother you?" Melody asked, suddenly concerned.

"Not one little bit," replied Dexter, giving her a comforting cuddle.

"I love you," Dexter said softly.

"I love you too," Melody quietly replied.

Dexter stood up and took Melody's hand. He led her into the bedroom, where they made love emotionally and gently. Their love grew as they moulded together; feelings were shared and souls were touched. It felt like the pure, unconditional love that Melody had always dreamed of. They both enjoyed a wonderful dinner that night in their room and slept entwined in each other's arms. When the sun arose the next morning, they awoke smiling at each other.

"Soul," said Melody.

"Soul," replied Dexter.

They stared into each other's eyes for what seemed like an eternity, caught up in the moment of pure love. Melody was lost in Dexter's eyes, and she felt that she could feel his soul.

After breakfast, they swam and played ball games in the ocean together, before retreating back to the hotel for a luxurious warm spa bath. They both knew this weekend would be etched in their memories forever.

Chapter Eleven

****

It had been raining for two days now, and it finally just stopped. Outside, everything was wet, muddy and waterlogged, and the children's playground at the bottom of the road was flooded and unusable.

Melody opened up her balcony doors to have a better look at the weather outside. "It's finally stopped raining!" she said. "Hallelujah!"

"It's not over yet, babe," replied Dexter.

Melody jumped back onto her bed again next to Dexter. They were lounging on her bed, snuggled up watching a movie. All of a sudden, there was a loud banging on the front door. They both jumped up in fright.

"I know he's in there! Where is he?" yelled a loud, booming voice.

"Oh no!" Melody gasped.

"Who's that?" asked Dexter worriedly.

"My ex-boyfriend! You better hide!" Melody told Dexter.

"Hide? I haven't done anything wrong," Dexter said, looking frustrated and annoyed.

"I'd still hide if I were you," she advised him. Her serious face worried Dexter.

"Oh my God. There's nowhere to hide!" he said.

"I can hear voices! Where is he?" Alex shouted. He was getting angrier and angrier, leading the couple to panic more and more.

Alex had been Melody's boyfriend previously for four years. He was a tall, thickly built man with a Canadian accent. He had moved over to New Zealand as a teenager with his family, but still sported a strong accent. Everyone liked Alex, as he was the life of the party, and Melody had loved how vivacious he was. He also liked to look after her. However, in fact, he looked after her on his credit card, which she paid off when they moved in together. So, in fact, she financed her own romantic courting in the end! Oh, he was so lazy in bed due to an extremely low libido, too. She wasn't entirely sure why she stayed with him, except that she was afraid of being left behind on the shelf at an old age!

She eventually told him she wanted to end their relationship. She just couldn't live like that anymore. It was the best decision she had ever made, and she had felt incredibly relieved when he'd moved out. He did take everything they'd bought together though. He didn't leave her anything! Even though he had been in and out of jobs and she was the main bread winner, he considered it was his right to take everything, as she had ended their relationship. Now, here he was on her doorstep again.

Melody quickly smoothed the covers on her bed and went downstairs. She met Alex at her front door. "Hello, Alex," Melody said in a deliberately calm voice.

"Let me in! Where is he?" boomed Alex.

"Where is who?" Melody replied, trying to keep her cool.

"I've heard you're seeing someone else already, and I can hear voices inside!" he yelled.

"Well, we've been separated for quite a while. That does mean I can actually see other people now," she told him firmly.

"Not yet, surely," he said.

"Look, I'll let you in if you calm down. There's no one else here. I was watching a movie upstairs. That must have been the voices you heard," she said.

Alex seemed to calm down, and Melody opened the door to let him in. Immediately, he ran upstairs three steps at a time and into Melody's bedroom.

"Where is he?!" he yelled.

Melody ran upstairs. But Dexter wasn't there, thankfully! Alex looked around. He looked behind the door, under the bed, in the guest room and all over the house. Dexter was nowhere to be seen.

"Oh, okay then, you are all alone," Alex sheepishly said, looking rather embarrassed.

"Yes, I am," Melody said, still making an effort to appear calm. "Do you mind if I enjoy my afternoon again, please?"

"Ah, okay," said Alex. Then, he promptly left like a dog with his tail between his legs.

Only when Melody heard his car drive away did

she run upstairs. *Where is Dexter?* When she entered her bedroom, she called out Dexter's name quietly. The door to her wardrobe slowly slid open, and there standing behind Melody's long flowing dresses was a very squashed Dexter. There were shoe boxes and shoes in front of him hiding his feet. He practically fell out of the cupboard he was so wedged in there.

"Has he gone?" asked Dexter. "I thought he was going to kill me!"

Melody just stood there and laughed! Dexter couldn't help but join in with her infectious laughter.

That was a close call!

Chapter Twelve

(Two Years Later)

****

Putting the phone down, Dexter faced his computer. He had just been speaking with a client about a new advertising campaign and was now waiting to hear back on their final approval before getting started.

Dexter had been working continually for this company for the last two years and was slowly rising within its ranks. His boss came and stood by his desk. "Dexter, have you got a minute?"

"Yes, of course," Dexter replied. He followed his boss into his extravagant office.

"Take a seat, please," his boss requested.

"Is everything okay?" Dexter asked nervously.

"Yes, everything is fine. Better than fine, actually. I've called you in to have a chat, because our

Sister Company in Hong Kong needs someone to manage a new advertising campaign. It's due to run for eight months. They need someone who is hands-on, proactive, energetic and can take the bull by the horns, so to speak. They are snowed under right now and need some help with this. If you're interested, there is a relocation package and a hefty salary to go with it. It will be brilliant experience, Dexter — what do you think?" his boss asked.

Dexter didn't say anything at first. He just looked at his boss while he let this information sink in. He admired the man in front of him, and he had become his mentor. Behind all his brash, loud talk, he was an astute businessman, and he had allowed Dexter to excel within the Company at a steady pace since he'd joined. *Sounds like a big break*, thought Dexter.

"Yes, I'll do it!" he replied.

"Excellent! I'm so happy to hear that, Dexter. I wanted to give you first option. Okay, you'll start there in one month's time," his boss said.

"In one month. That's quick! Can I take Melody with me?" Dexter requested.

"Yes, I don't see why not. She won't be able to

work, though, but you'll be able to take her along with you," he answered. "See Tonya; she'll organise your passport documentation and will give you all the details of your relocation and salary package. I'm sure you'll be very happy." He smiled.

They both stood up and shook hands. "Thank you very much," said Dexter, feeling a buzz of excitement.

Dexter went back to his seat with a smile on his face and ambition in his pocket. He thought about Melody. He couldn't imagine being away from her for eight months. He sincerely hoped she would come along to Hong Kong for the ride.

Chapter Thirteen

****

Dexter and Melody's relationship had continued to blossom over the two years since they met. During that time, they moved into an apartment together, and it felt like home. They furnished it with modern and sleek furniture, with abundant plants growing indoors giving it a natural feel. The large earth coloured fluffy cushions on the sofa in the lounge room, made it feel cosy and homely. They were settled and loved living together. The bond they shared was true, loving and supportive. Their relationship was as solid as a rock.

They had just finished cooking a tasty meal of Hungarian Goulash with rice together, accompanied by a glass of Cabernet Sauvignon. Dexter had already prepared a table and two chairs on the balcony outside. There they sat, dining under the stars, watching the lights of the Auckland city skyline twinkle in front of them. The Sky Tower looked radiant as it dominated their night view. The night was clear and the stars were vast and numerous. It was a magical sight. They clinked their wine glasses together, and both sipped the alcohol whilst looking into each other's eyes.

"Cheers," said Dexter as they clinked wine glasses.

"Cheers," replied Melody, smiling. "This feels like a special dinner tonight."

"Well, it just so happens, it is a special night," said Dexter.

"Really? Why?" Melody asked.

"I was offered an amazing opportunity today at work," said Dexter a little nervously.

"Oh wow, what was it?" Melody inquired.

"I've been asked to work in Hong Kong for eight months, to run an advertising campaign," said Dexter.

"Eight months!" replied Melody, sounding a little shocked. "Oh, that sounds wonderful, but I'll miss you." Melody wasn't sure if she was happy or sad.

"But there's good news. I can take you too!" Dexter

said excitedly, holding Melody's hand.

"Oh wow! Really?" Melody said in surprise. "What would I do there? Can I work?" she asked.

"No, it's not possible for you to work there, but you can have an adventure with me," he replied. "Maybe we could go on a travel expedition afterwards as well?"

"Now, that sounds exciting!" she said. "So I'll have to quit my job then?"

"Probably," replied Dexter.

Melody thought about this proposal. It reminded her of her days as a travel agent, and the idea of travelling overseas again brought back many happy memories. Focusing on this thought, she made her decision.

"Yes," she said, squeezing his hand, "I'd love to!"

They hugged enthusiastically and their legs danced with excitement.

"Guess what, babe?" yelled Dexter.

"What?" asked Melody, feeling that she couldn't get any more excited.

"It comes with a big, fat salary as well!" Dexter smiled.

"Yay!" said Melody, hugging Dexter again. She didn't feel that she could be any happier.

Chapter Fourteen

****

As they approached Hong Kong in their taxi from the airport, Melody could feel the exhilaration of the city. Every city she had ever visited overseas had its own distinct feel, its own electrical stamp, and Hong Kong was a live wire. It looked and felt vibrant and intoxicating.

The taxi weaved through a myriad of streets, past trams and huge crowds of people leaving work for the day. Melody's senses were tweaked by the numerous advertising signs. There were hordes of them on top of each other, all vying for a place to be seen. They were suspended over the road, and Melody felt surrounded by English and Chinese characters and the stunning Chinese people staring out from the boards. It wasn't like anything she had ever seen before. As they drove, they were bombarded by the vast arrangements of music coming from the shops and stalls, which interchanged as they drove past one shop and then moved on past another. Hong Kong was a mixture of the past, present and future. Futuristic new buildings were being built with bamboo scaffolding attached to the sides. Melody thought it was such a contradiction.

It was certainly the place to be in marketing. There was marketing everywhere! Every little bit of inner city real estate had a billboard of some kind. It was crazy and colourful.

Melody squeezed Dexter's hand, and he squeezed her hand back. They were both sucked into the sights of Hong Kong from the back of the taxi. Their mouths opened as they watched the buzzing streets. They were speechless.

Melody had never felt more alive. She loved being surrounded by this concoction of sensory delights. She knew how lucky she was to be included on this journey with Dexter, and she was going to be by his side every step of the way. Her heart burst with love and pride for the man who sat next to her.

The taxi pulled to the side of the road halfway up a hill. They had finally arrived at their apartment complex, which was to be their home for the next eight months.

"This is so exciting!" exclaimed Dexter.

"It sure is! I wonder what adventures and fun times we'll have," replied Melody.

They walked towards their apartment building, past groups of people talking to each other in a language they couldn't understand.

Dexter squeezed Melody's hand again before opening the entrance door for her.

Chapter Fifteen

****

Their apartment was in an area called Happy Valley, and the building was built on the side of a steep hill. The whole street was, in fact, made up of apartment buildings. Melody thought it must have been quite an engineering feat building so many apartments on this hill. She certainly hoped everybody in the building lived up to the name 'Happy Valley!' Wheeling their suitcases inside, they took the elevator to the sixth floor and found room 24A. As they walked through the corridor, it felt like being in a hotel. When they opened the front door to their apartment, they were surprised at the luxury in front of them. An affluent three-bedroom apartment with stunning views across the Race Course awaited them.

There was one word that described the apartment: 'modern.' It was huge by Hong Kong standards, and everything seemed shiny. The tiles on the floor, the smooth kitchen cupboards, the dining room table top — everything was 'shiny'. The object that Melody loved as soon as she walked in was the thick, cream-coloured, shaggy rug on the lounge room floor. It made the room look warm and inviting. The plants dotted around the apartment softened the modern look and gave it a homely feel. With much enthusiasm, they both investigated the rooms. They sat on the edge of the bed in the main bedroom testing the mattress, flopped on the couch in the lounge room, and turned the taps on in the bathroom. The apartment had passed the 'comfy' test.

Melody and Dexter then sat down on the couch in the lounge room, looking out of the large window.

"Look at the view!" said Melody.

"We don't need to go to the Race Course; we can place bets from up here!" Dexter replied, laughing.

"We could make up names for the horses. What would you call your horse?" asked Melody.

"Hhhhmmmm...How about, *Better Late Than Never?*" Dexter laughed. "What about yours?"

"Hhhmmmm...I think the way I'm feeling right now, I would call it, *Am I Dreaming?*" Melody laughed.

"Should I pinch you then?" said Dexter, laughing and chasing her off the sofa and around the apartment with pinching crab claw hands.

Melody ran around until she flopped on the bed in the main bedroom. Dexter jumped on the bed and pretended to pinch her all over. They laughed together and embraced on the large, comfortable bed.

Both of them were excited about the next eight months.

Chapter Sixteen

****

The next day, they awoke at 11am. Their pizza boxes were still strewn on the dining table, along with their dirty glasses. They were so exhausted after their long-haul flight they fell into bed after dinner and slept soundly. Their apartment was incredibly quiet and they couldn't hear any of their neighbours. They secretly wondered if anyone else lived on their floor. It was eerily quiet.

Dexter was wading through his suitcase, trying to find a pair of socks, as Melody was in the bathroom brushing her teeth. "I'm starving!" he called through to her.

"Me too!" replied Melody after rinsing her mouth out. "I guess we should find a supermarket?"

"I don't have time for that; I need to have food right now," replied Dexter, half-joking, half-serious. "I am starving," he said again.

"I have an idea. When in Hong Kong, what shall

we eat for breakfast? Yum Cha!" suggested Melody. "I'm sure we passed a restaurant not far from here when we arrived yesterday."

"I'm up for that," said Dexter eagerly. "Let's go. I'm going to start eating the walls soon!"

After a quick clean-up, the couple left the apartment and headed down the hill to the restaurant. When they found it, they walked through the entrance and followed the signs to the third floor. The smell as they entered seemed to beckon them further inside. It smelled delicious!

No sooner had they been escorted to a table, than the Yum Cha carts were wheeled their way. The food looked delightful and they'd never eaten Yum Cha like it before. The sweet pork buns had been given cute pink ears and a snout, which had been crafted out of flour dough and edible eyes. The custard buns also had edible eyes on top. It was the weirdest and most creative Yum Cha either of them had seen, and they ate it quickly and with great pleasure.

Later in the day, they shopped at the nearby supermarket and stocked their apartment with an array of tasty necessities. They unpacked their suitcases and stored them in the spare room. By the end of the day, their apartment looked lived in and like their own.

Satisfied, they collapsed on the sofa with a lemon, lime and vodka.

"This place feels like home already," said Melody.

"It sure does," replied Dexter. "You know what, let's go out. I've heard about a place called The Peak, and it's supposed to have awesome views of Hong Kong. Shall we go and have a look?" asked Dexter.

"That sounds like fun," said Melody, finishing her drink.

They hailed a taxi not far from their apartment and drove to the Peak Tram Station. There was a crowd out the front of the station, and they had to line up for thirty minutes. Eventually, they climbed on board the tram to begin their ascent to The Peak. After the departure tram announcement, the tram slowly started to pull away very smoothly. Almost immediately, the tram tilted to a steep angle as they climbed up the mountain, and soon they rode away from the buildings and were surrounded by trees. Melody was surprised to see how many palm trees were growing in this area. After only ten minutes on the tram, they arrived at the station on The Peak.

"That was amazing!" said Dexter.

"Wow," said Melody. "The journey up the peak... it was so steep. It made the apartment buildings look like they were leaning towards the mountain and were about to slide down," said Melody. "Did it feel like that for you too?"

"It did!" said Dexter. "It was a very weird sensation! I read about that illusion in the magazine on the plane flying over here," said Dexter. "Let's go find the look out." Dexter stopped at a map. "It's called the Sky Terrace and it's this way." He pointed left.

They took an escalator higher than they already were and walked through some shops before finally exiting the station. The night was closing in and it was getting dark. Melody buttoned up her light jacket to keep warm. Dexter took her by her hand and they walked to the Sky Terrace.

"Look at the view, Dex!" Melody announced as they approached the viewing station. The sight below them was nothing short of magical. The multitudes of skyscrapers were lit up, and they shimmered and glistened in the night. Victoria Harbour was illuminated by the sparkle of the surrounding buildings, and the Hong Kong ferries provided a moving, magical picture. Melody and Dexter snuggled into each other's arms.

"Thank you so much for bringing me with you, Dexter," whispered Melody, still spellbound by their surroundings.

"You're welcome. I couldn't imagine being here without you," replied Dexter.

"How are you feeling about your first day in the office tomorrow?" asked Melody.

"Excited and very nervous. But, I'm looking forward to it, mainly," Dexter said.

"You'll do great. I'll be there in spirit with you, babe," Melody said encouragingly.

Dexter looked into Melody's eyes, then kissed her. He felt like he could take on the world with his girl by his side.

Chapter Seventeen

****

Over the next eight months, Melody and Dexter lived a good life. Melody learnt Mandarin and Dexter excelled at delivering his advertising campaign at work. Melody mentored him and gave him the confidence to deliver, and he came to depend on her from the sidelines. They were a strong couple and their relationship continued to grow.

Weekends were busy within the expat community, and they were often out enjoying drinks with new friends and dining on long, lavish dinners. Melody and Dexter enjoyed experiencing everything Hong Kong had to offer. They visited countless tourist stops like Mong Kok Market, Stanley Market, Hong Kong Disneyland and Lamma Island, and went hiking. They especially enjoyed the trek to the Ten Thousand Buddhas Monastery in the Sha Tin New Territories. Their legs did pay for it the next day, though, after tackling four hundred and thirty steps to get there!

By the time their eight months was over, they had participated in nearly every tourist experience in Hong Kong. Melody had also enjoyed her Mandarin studies and Dexter had completed his advertising campaign astutely. It was an incredible experience and one they would never forget.

After leaving Hong Kong, Melody and Dexter embarked on further adventures and travelled to Cambodia, Indonesia, Japan, Venezuela, Colombia and Great Britain.

All too soon, it was time to return to Auckland for Easter, but oh, what an adventure they'd had.

Chapter Eighteen

****

Like any couple, or in fact any single person, who has travelled the world, the travel bubble burst when Melody and Dexter returned home, leaving them with a bit of a crash. But they lived in a homely apartment in a beautiful city, and they had Easter to look forward to. Their moods soon lifted as they prepared for the festivities.

On Easter Sunday, Dexter's family all came together, inclusive of wives and girlfriends, and they congregated at his parents' home. He was one of four children, all of whom were there. Melody's parents lived near Ashburton on their farm, which is on the South Island, so she joined Dexter's family.

Melody could see Dexter's parents' home well before they had arrived, as there was a beautiful tall Kauri tree in their front garden. His parents owned a huge family home, and they had lived there for almost twenty years. Melody could feel the memories seeped within the walls, and she admired the arrangement of family portraits and photos on their dining room wall.

It was noisy in the house, as everyone was talking at the same time. His mother, Roseanne, who was a sturdy and robust woman, was working in the kitchen, and all the ladies were helping her. It was a traditional arrangement, as the women would prepare the Easter Sunday lunch and the men would chat whilst waiting. Secretly, this did worry Melody, as she was wary of any man from such a traditional family. However, knowing Dexter as she did, she quickly forgot about her concerns.

Harold was Dexter's father, and he enjoyed watering his garden whilst drinking a beer at the same time. He was a tall man with a rotund belly and he had a good head of hair for a man his age. He loved his family wholeheartedly and always seemed relaxed and jovial.

When Melody and Dexter arrived, Harold gave them a warm hug, and Roseanne came out to greet both of them.

"Come in, come in!" the parents said.

They sat down as lunch was being placed on the

table. Easter Sunday lunch was roast pork with crackle on the side. The roasted vegetables were piled high on a large plate in the middle of the table, and there was a separate super-large bowl of greens accompanied by stuffed mushrooms and another bowl of applesauce for the pork. It was a magnificent spread.

"Ahhhhhh, that smells amazing, Mum," said Dexter.

"It does smell tasty! What a superb Easter feast, ladies! Let's dig in everyone. Happy Easter!" boomed Harold.

"Happy Easter!" everybody heartily replied.

As they ate, the table buzzed with conversation, jokes, laughter, and the cluttering of utensils. Afterwards, the ladies were in the kitchen cleaning up, the young children were running all over the house and the men were examining Harold's fish pond he'd dug out himself in the rear garden. It was a real work of suburban art!

Melody loved visiting and she loved Dexter's family. She was considered a part of his family.

But something was missing for her...

Chapter Nineteen

****

Melody and Dexter soon settled back into a routine of love, fun, work, friends and family commitments. However, it wasn't long before they started to get itchy feet as they yearned to travel again. Something didn't feel right to Melody, though. She was now 38 years old, and she wished and hoped for a family. Dexter was just 27. They had never had a conversation about how important having a family was for Melody. She tried to ignore the instinct that told her that having children wasn't important to him.

Could love conquer all?

Four months after they arrived back in Auckland, the couple sat down to a home-cooked dinner. Melody had lovingly prepared honey stir-fried chicken and egg noodles.

"Hey, Dex, can I discuss something with you?" she asked as she swirled her fork around her plate.

"Sure, what's up?" replied Dexter. He slurped a noodle into his mouth.

"Well, it's not easy for me to say this, so I'm just going to blurt it out..." Melody took a deep breath, then resumed. "We've had such an amazing time together... But, well, the clock's ticking," she said. "I'm getting older and my feelings to have a family keep getting stronger. This is something I need to do. I don't want to miss the opportunity to experience being a mother. I feel so strongly about this," she said.

She was looking into her dinner. She didn't dare look up at Dexter. She knew deep down that her feelings were far removed from where Dexter was at this stage in his life. Eventually, she looked up and over at him. He laid his fork sideways on his plate and stared at her with a slightly open mouth.

"Wow!" he said. "I just didn't think..."

"I've felt this way for a while now, but I was too afraid to tell you my feelings," Melody replied.

"Would you wait until I felt ready?" Dexter asked. He picked up his fork again and poked at his noodles.

"How long would that be?" asked Melody. She knew that anything he said would be too long.

"Oh," Dexter paused for too long. "I don't know," he finally said. He put his fork down again. He'd lost his appetite.

Melody felt tears welling in her eyes, which she tried to fight. "You know, I don't want to say this, Dex, but I can't keep going on like this. I really want to find someone to have a family with."

Dexter shook his head, whilst Melody continued.

"I love you," she said. A tear rolled down her cheek as she looked into Dexter's shining, green eyes. "I've had an amazing few years with you, but, b-"

"No, no, Melody," Dexter said, putting his hand on hers. "We don't need to end things."

They both sat in silence. Melody picked up her glass of red wine and drained it. Suddenly, Dexter remembered something.

"There is a guy at work who had IVF with his wife," he began. "His wife is pregnant now, but they still have embryos which are frozen. They're planning on using them to get pregnant with their second child," he said. He held onto Melody's hand and looked into her eyes. She'd stopped crying.

"I don't want to lose you," he said gently. "I love you so much. You mean the world to me. We can have a family; I want to have a family with you! Just not yet. I'm not ready, Melody," he said.

Melody nodded. Without knowing it, she touched her stomach. "So," she said, "we can freeze our embryos? We can start our family that way, soon?"

"We can start our family that way, right away." Dexter smiled.

Chapter Twenty

****

Dexter sat on the couch after dinner while Melody had a shower. He was completely rattled by their conversation at dinner tonight. The 'baby' topic had been completely out of the blue and he felt thoroughly unprepared for such a subject. *A baby,* he thought.... He just couldn't picture himself being a father now or in the future. He truly didn't know if he ever wanted children. When he looked at his older work colleagues and heard them talking about their children, it seemed to him they were a constant burden. *Would he ever be ready for that?*

What he did know was that he loved having Melody in his life. She gave him the strength he needed and her presence made him feel complete. Melody had helped to guide him in the right direction in Hong Kong and always put everything into perspective when he was stressed about work. Dexter felt more of a man with her by his side, and he wanted to keep her right there. He wanted to travel overseas again and take the next step in his career, and he knew he could only do that with Melody.

It wouldn't hurt to go along with this IVF, he thought.

They could freeze some embryos, which would keep Melody happy. It would also give him the option to become a father, when he was ready. "It is a win/win plan," he told himself.

He walked into the kitchen and poured himself a glass of cabernet sauvignon.

Chapter Twenty-One

****

Melody was in awe of Dexter's suggestion. She thought that the foresight showed real maturity on his behalf. So, that was their plan. They would create some embryos and freeze them, so Melody could postpone motherhood until Dexter was ready.

That was it, decided.

******

As they sat in the consultation room discussing a myriad of tests, procedures and IVF success rates with the doctor, Melody felt detached. The doctor's voice seemed slower than usual and Dexter seemed to be on a completely different planet.

"This is quite an unusual family planning route," said Dr White. "If you don't mind me asking, what's the reason for your not having children now?"

"We're in a relationship and have been for a number of years," Melody said.

"But Melody is eleven years older than me," Dexter interrupted quickly. "We're trying to put motherhood on hold until we are both ready." He leant back in his chair, looking a little too relaxed for the doctor's liking.

Dr White looked directly at Dexter. "You're not ready to have a family, but your partner is?" he asked calmly.

"That's right," replied Dexter, reaching out to squeeze Melody's hand.

Dr White then looked back to Melody. "If you're trying to put motherhood on hold, have you considered freezing your eggs?" he said.

"No, I've not actually contemplated that," replied Melody. Melody thought to herself, *That's actually not a bad idea!*

"No," said Dexter, suddenly defensive. "We're doing this together. I want to freeze embryos for the both of us."

After Dr White confirmed with the couple that this was exactly what they wanted, they booked the first run of tests and agreed to have a second consultation in several weeks' time.

Dexter and Melody left the surgery, hand in hand and smiling. Both felt like winners.

Chapter Twenty-Two

****

Melody suddenly found herself the subject of further tests, a barrage of injections and, to top it all off, nasal sprays. She routinely attended all the consultations and became used to the intermittent ultrasounds to check how her ovaries were coping and how many eggs she would produce. She was taking a concoction of injections and medications to help her to produce more eggs than she normally would naturally. Possibly, from one of those, a beautiful child would be born.

Hopefully, just hopefully…

Finally, Melody and Dexter were ready to create embryos together.

On their first and only attempt, they created seven healthy embryos. That wasn't a lot, but Melody thought that would be enough. She only wanted to have two children anyway!

She was surprised by how immediately she felt

connected to her embryos, almost like she was a mother in some form already. She couldn't dispel this maternal feeling that was ripe within her now, and her excitement was real at the prospect of holding her own little baby one day.

She wished she didn't have to wait, but she did find it comforting to know they were there waiting for her. This knowledge didn't stop the question nagging in her mind, "How long would they be in the freezer?"

Chapter Twenty-Three

****

Now that their family plans had successfully been placed on hold, Dexter and Melody were contemplating their next adventure as a couple.

Still riding high on the memories of their travelling expedition and living in Hong Kong, they started to consider moving to London in the United Kingdom to live. The prospect of earning big money in the marketing industry was what lured Dexter, whilst Melody was keen to experience a new culture. She found the thought of living and working abroad incredibly exciting. After work, they sat on their garden chairs on their balcony with a lemon, lime and vodka to discuss their vision.

"You know, babe, my friend Marcus returned back from London last month. He bought a Ferrari after working in London," Dexter said. His excitement was visible as his eyes shined even brighter than usual.

"Oh my goodness! That's amazing!" Melody said. She looked excited, too, and more carefree than she'd been in recent weeks.

"We could make lots of money over a couple of years and come back and buy a house outright," Dexter said. "Imagine that!" he added. "Think of the life we could live there as well, and all the clothes we could buy!" he said.

"That does sound incredibly tempting," said Melody. She was, of course, thinking about children.

She fantasized about their own house: a beautiful, modern, clean and spacious house. She imagined a playroom, with a little girl in it. Or a little boy. Or perhaps both...

She looked up at Dexter again and smiled. She admired his energy and determination. He craved financial success, and what family man wouldn't? She imagined him driving their children to parties, in a convertible car.

"What do you think, babe?" Dexter interrupted her fantasies. "We could have an amazing life together, if we do this. London. Shall we do it?"

"Let's," Melody said. "Let's go to London!"

Chapter Twenty-Four

****

Before they knew it, Melody and Dexter were packing their belongings into storage. It seemed like seconds later that they were saying goodbye to friends and family, then boarding the plane. Melody had felt intensely excited about the future. She felt that this journey was the beginning of another chapter in her and Dexter's life.

She had friends in Shepherds Bush, West London, who they could stay with initially. Annisa, an ex work-colleague and her husband, Robert. They'd kindly offered to let her and Dexter stay in their apartment until they found a place of their own.

After they'd stayed for a couple of nights at Annisa and Robert's, Melody started to look for an apartment for her and Dexter to live in. Dexter stayed behind and applied for marketing jobs on the Internet. Melody always did the groundwork, whilst Dexter worked on his own career.

She felt slightly irritated as she travelled all over

London visiting a multitude of apartments and talking with various estate agents. It was a brilliant way to get to know the city, though! London was vibrant and stimulating. However, it was proving impossible to rent an apartment on their own until they were actually working. No one would give them a chance, not without proof that they were currently in employment.

After many visits to a variety of agents, Melody walked into an estate agency in Wimbledon. The receptionist was a young lady and she must have been around twenty years old. She looked extremely confident for her age, and her face was expertly made up.

"Hi, I'm interested in renting the apartment in Arthur Road," Melody said to the receptionist.

"Okay, we can take you to have a look, if you like," replied the receptionist. "Are you currently working?"

"No, my boyfriend and I have just arrived from New Zealand. We'll be working soon, but we just need to find somewhere to live now," Melody answered. "We can show you proof of savings."

"Ah, that's good. But we need to see proof of employment for both of you as well," the receptionist advised.

"So there's no way we can rent an apartment at present?" Melody asked.

"I'm afraid not," the receptionist replied. "Have you considered shared accommodation?" she asked.

"Well, I think we'll have to," Melody said.

Melody returned to Annisa and Robert's place and shared the news with Dexter. That night, they both searched the Internet together for shared accommodation. They quickly found a room for rent on the other side of Shepherds Bush.

They went to see the apartment together the next day, and hastily decided to take it. It was a brilliant five-bedroom apartment with modern appliances and it was close to many transport links. They moved in the next day. The apartment was on the middle floor of the building and, including Melody and Dexter, there were eight people living there. The apartment benefited from some brilliant views, and on Guy Fawkes Night, they could see many different fireworks displays across London, in the surrounding boroughs.

However, due to the uncleanliness of some of the occupants, it was the kind of shared apartment where flip-flops needed to be worn in the communal areas. Especially the kitchen, which Melody hardly dared prepare food in. But she and Dexter agreed that it was an interesting place to live. The six flatmates were all Romanians, and they smoked marijuana frequently. Melody and Dexter had to keep their clothes and washing in their bedroom with the door closed to keep them from smelling like the weed. Sometimes, Melody could smell the marijuana through the keyhole before she even unlocked the front door. She and Dexter both became quite relaxed about finding a job and living in a new country, which they jokily put down to passively smoking the weed.

Melody started temping work straight away, working in different businesses as an administrator, personal assistant and as a receptionist. She earned money to pay for their expenses, whilst Dexter was still looking for a job. It was four months before he started work in the marketing industry. During those four months, Melody worked hard. She travelled to all ends of London for work. Sometimes, she travelled three hours in total to and from work in one day. She was totally exhausted by Friday each week.

Melody remembered looking after Dexter in Hong Kong whilst he was working. She did absolutely everything for him. But right now, she was working so hard in London, and not once did he make her lunch or do anything domestic to help. She still had to do everything for both of them, by herself. She tried not to let it get her down, guessing it was the traditional family influence.

They both found London to be hard work. The crowding and rudeness in the peak hour train ride to and from work were alien to them. There was nowhere they could go to escape from people. They got used to the lack of privacy, though, and at least they were both working after the initial four months.

After eight months in London, Dexter moved into a new marketing position. He started earning decent money, but it was never enough for him. They both scrimped, scraped and saved any way they could. Dexter made Melody feel guilty if she bought anything new for herself, and they took minimal holidays. They went to pubs for dinner or to restaurants offering two-for-one main meal deals. Not once did they go to a beautiful restaurant. He also frowned upon getting into rounds at bars. Melody was exhausted! This was not the promised life Dexter had enticed her with.

But, it was a city where she made some amazing friends. She contracted around London, and as she did, she collected friends in each place she worked. Some of these friendships would last a lifetime.

Although this wasn't what Dexter had sold to her, Melody still felt they were working together towards something special. They were building up a nest egg for their children that were very patiently waiting. That thought kept her going.

Chapter Twenty-Five

****

After 18 months in London, Melody began to plan for Dexter's 30th birthday. As well as looking for presents for him, though, she needed to speak to him. They'd been saving for a while together, but they hadn't talked about why. Surely, it was for their children. Wasn't it?

"Hey, babe, can I talk to you for a minute?" asked Melody.

Dexter typed into his laptop. He didn't make eye contact with Melody as he responded. "Sure," he said.

"Well, you know how we have children frozen. I'd love to make a plan for when we're going to have our family." She smiled at him.

Dexter looked at Melody briefly, then turned back to his screen. "Well, I'm still not ready," he said.

Melody's face dropped into a frown. "Do you have

any idea when you're going to be ready?"

"No, I don't. I thought I would be by now, but I'm just not ready," he said. "I'm sorry," he added.

Melody said nothing as she turned away from Dexter.

"I don't know if I'll ever be ready," he added.

Melody stared at him. She perched on the edge of the sofa. "What do you mean?" she said.

"I just don't know if I want a family," he said, matter-of-factly. There was guilt in his eyes, but he looked relieved to be getting the words out.

Melody couldn't believe what she was hearing.

"Melody," Dexter said, "I'm going to go away for a couple of days. I need some time to think. I need to reflect, alone."

"Okay," said Melody, trying once again to stop tears falling. "Is it something I've done?" she asked, as her voice broke.

"No, nothing at all," replied Dexter. He was still staring at his laptop screen, refusing to look in Melody's direction.

Dexter went away the following weekend. He didn't say where to, and Melody didn't ask. She spent the time alone, in and out of tears. Her fantasies of their future family were suddenly less vivid.

Chapter Twenty-Six

****

Dexter watched the countryside whizz by on the train to Brighton. He'd arranged to stay with his friend, Edmund from work. Edmund was a charming Englishman, but his behaviour did tend to change considerably after a pint or four. After a few drinks, he became loud and cocky, though still – Dexter thought – entertaining.

Like Dexter, Edmund had blond hair, though his was beginning to grey. He was a little shorter than Dexter. Edmund had recently broken up with his wife of ten years. She left, saying that she'd had enough of his nightly drinking. He was angry and bitter after their breakup, and often complained about being 'forced' to pay child maintenance, to help look after his two little girls. He was a distant father, who rarely spoke to his girls and would never hug them. He always referred to them as 'the child' or 'the children', rarely calling them by their names. After Dexter confided in Edmund one night after work about his conversation with Melody, Edmund suggested he stayed with him for the weekend.

The train pulled into Brighton Station and Dexter stepped out onto the platform. Edmund was there waiting for Dexter at the ticket barrier. They shook hands in a friendly yet semi-formal manner, then headed to the nearest pub. Edmund bought them both a pint, then started the conversation.

"So, Dexter, what are your worries?" he said.

Dexter opened up immediately. "I want to be with Melody," he said, "but I just don't know if I'm ready to have children."

Edmund nodded. "Okay," he said. "Well, it's a huge commitment, and one you bloody well better be ready for!" He curled his lip.

"When you had children, how did you feel?" asked Dexter, looking at the older man in admiration. Although he was clearly bitter, he looked knowledgeable, wise...

"Well, it just happened," Edmund said. "I don't think I was ever ready to be a father. My missus looked after the children and I only saw them on weekends. They were always in bed by the time I got home on weekdays. All I know is that they're damn expensive!" he said.

"Oh, okay," replied Dexter. He thought about the savings he'd worked so hard to start building.

"Look, have you lived your life yet?" Edmund said. "When you have children, everything changes. Your old life just disappears."

Dexter looked down. "Well, if I'm honest with myself, sometimes I feel like I need to experience more," he said. "Melody is eleven years older than me, and we met when I was young..."

"Ah, you want to get out and sow your oats!" Edmund laughed.

"You know, maybe I do!" Dexter laughed. "I find New Zealand girls so damn boring now! When I look around London, there are girls from Sweden, France, Italy and Germany. I want to try them all!" Dexter laughed. He bought them both another pint.

"Maybe you do need to get out there," Edmund said, after thanking Dexter for their second pint.

Dexter sipped his beer thoughtfully. "You know," he said, "Melody helps me make sound decisions. I want to set myself up here and she can help me to do that." He seemed to be calming down.

"You only get one life," said Edmund, less than calmly. "If you have children with this girl, and then in time you want to break up, she will be a ball and chain. You'll be the one paying money out for any little brat offspring you create for years. I regret having children now!"

His lips really curled now as he spoke. "You need to fend for yourself," he said, staring Dexter in the eye. "No one else will."

After a long pause, during which they both downed nearly half a pint, Edmund asked, "What is it you want to set up, anyway?"

"I want to buy a house here," Dexter said. "We're currently in shared accommodation, which is awful. Melody would be able to sort all of that out," he said. "It's hard in my job to find time to look for one."

Edmund breathed out heavily. "Okay. So here's what you do. Let her think you want to stay with her, find your house and buy it, then, after a few months, say you want to split up. She won't be able to afford the mortgage on her own, so you can pay her a daft amount of money to buy her out and put the house in your name solely. Easy peasy, then you're free of having little brats and you can play hanky-panky with the Swedish!" Edmund said, finishing his pint.

"That seems callous," said Dexter. He was more sober than Edmund, who he suspected had started drinking before they met.

"Well, it's your life! She is free to make her own decisions," Edmund said. "Seriously, did she think a relationship with a man eleven years younger than her would actually work? Seems like she's living in a dreamland to me! Maybe she's taking advantage of you, Dexter? Have you ever thought of that?"

Dexter shook his head. "What do you mean?" he asked.

"Well, you brought her over here to London. Maybe she was just keen to get out of New Zealand? You were her ticket out of there," said Edmund. "So the question is, 'Who is going to use who?' If you stay with her, you will have a child you don't want, and then when you break up, you will have to pay maintenance forever," Edmund said. "If I were you, I would go into damage control, get what you can and get out as easily as you can."

Dexter had never looked at this perspective before

and he could see exactly where Edmund was coming from. Their conversation returned to this topic time and time again throughout the weekend.

A seed had been planted...

Chapter Twenty-Seven

****

Dexter came back on Sunday night, and Melody met him at the door. She looked worried and shrunken, whilst Dexter somehow looked taller and even more confident than before he'd left. He wrapped his arms around and hugged her. She felt better: he still loved her. They were going to be okay.

Dexter led Melody into the lounge room and gestured to her to sit down. He seemed manlier, somehow. More authoritative. More... fatherly? She sat down, then he sat beside her.

"Melody," he said, "I love you so much, but I'm not ready to have a family yet. I know that I will be, though. Can you wait just a little longer? Just one more year?" He didn't break eye contact with her as he spoke.

Melody ignored how different he seemed and allowed herself to think about his proposal. She remembered all the special memories they shared together, all their adventures. She thought about the children they'd created: the little, frozen embryos and fantasized again about the future prospect of bringing up a loving family together. *I just need to be a little more patient,* she thought to herself.

"Yes, I can wait one more year," she said, smiling. "I love you," she continued, stroking Dexter's leg.

Just one more year, Melody thought. *One more year. It will fly, here in London.*

Chapter Twenty-Eight

****

Throughout the next year, Melody and Dexter both continued to work hard. They spent six months looking for the perfect house, before finally buying a beautiful home together in Hampstead Heath, London. It was comfortable, with bountiful space for bringing up a family. There was a wonderful area for socialising, which was light and airy, with large French doors opening out onto a patio. This room was a sun trap, letting in copious amounts of sunshine. It had a huge garden and a garage attached to the house for one car. Melody couldn't believe that they owned it. She could almost see their children playing in the garden. A year had almost passed. This was happening; this was really happening!

But even though that seemed to be, Melody sensed that there was something wrong. Dexter was slowly changing. His sun-bleached hair had become darker and he had grown a beard. He kept it trimmed and stylish, but it made him look older and... different. The beard made him seem strangely more distant. As though he was hiding behind the hair.

It wasn't just his appearance that had altered. He spoke to Melody less than ever and seemed increasingly withdrawn. It wasn't until they'd been in their new home for several weeks that Dexter finally struck up a serious conversation with Melody.

"I'm sorry, Melody," he said, as they finished their dinner together in silence one evening.

"I'm never going to be ready to have a family." The words fell from his mouth so easily.

"I didn't know I would feel this way, but our timing is all wrong. I don't want to have children with you now or next year," Dexter told her, picking their plates up and carrying them to the kitchen.

Melody felt sick. Her stomach felt as though it had been punched and her heart was in her throat. "What does that mean?" she said, as she followed him into the kitchen. She was afraid of the answer: afraid of the reality.

"I don't think I'm the person for you. I just can't see myself having children, and I couldn't expect you to stay with me because of that," Dexter said.

He didn't seem to care, which is what was hurting Melody the most.

"But we've been building a dream together," she replied. She felt desperate, angry and betrayed.

"I'm really sorry," Dexter said. She thought that she spotted regret in his eyes as he said that, until he continued, "But I need to live my life now on my own for a while."

"So you want to be with other women?" Melody said, half-gasping as she struggled to speak.

"Yes, I suppose you could put it that way," he replied.

Melody burst into tears. "What about our children?" she cried. Tears were falling down her face and she could hardly breathe.

"What about them?" Dexter said.

"We've had IVF, we created and committed to having children together," Melody cried. Snot was falling into her mouth.

Dexter remained composed. "Yes, I did at the time, but I've changed my mind now," he said. "I don't want to any more. I'm sorry, Melody."

Melody felt overwhelmed with sadness. She was about to turn 41 years old and she had waited over six years for this man. This boy. This pathetic, selfish boy!

"I want you to move out," he said.

Melody couldn't believe that the blows were still coming. "What?" She said. Anger was taking over her sadness now. "WHAT?" She shouted. "This is MY HOME TOO!"

"Yes, but you can't afford the mortgage by yourself; you will have to move out," said Dexter.

Melody felt as though she were in a bad dream. "What is WRONG WITH YOU?!" She shouted. "Only last night you said that you loved me!"

It was as she said that, that it dawned on her. Ever since they had arrived here, he had been pulling away from her. Just two days ago, she had helped him move his desk from the lounge room into their bedroom so he could work there. He'd been trying to stay out of her way. It was as plain as day, he had been preparing for this. Melody had stopped crying, but she felt ill. She had only just planted daffodil bulbs in the back garden, ready for Spring next year. She knew that she wouldn't be here to watch them grow. This never was going to be a long-term family home for the both of them. Dexter had manipulated and used her.

Melody's tears started falling again as she ran up to their bedroom. She slammed the door shut and lay face-first on their bed. She saw images of their beautiful children crumbling, deteriorating, then fading away before her eyes. She had waited such a long time. For what?

It became apparent to her on that day that...

Love does not conquer all.

Chapter Twenty-Nine

****

They slept in separate rooms for the next week as Melody tried to keep out of Dexter's way. When their paths did inevitably collide, he became cruel.

"I want you to get out."

"I'm not leaving this house until I buy my own place," Melody said with forced strength. "I deserve that," she added. "I've worked just as hard as you in London. Not to mention doing most of the work when it came to finding this place."

Melody needed Dexter's help to buy a property, as she needed access to their joint funds. When he broke up with her, her pay had just been automatically transferred into their joint bank account. As she was now in-between contracts, she had absolutely no money of her own. Dexter warned her not to touch their joint bank account. Until she started a new contract again, she had no money for food or transport. Absolutely nothing.

She felt incredibly helpless and trapped, yet Dexter told her repeatedly to leave. To where?

It was after she'd overheard him talking to his mother on the phone that he finally showed hints of empathy. He offered to help her buy a small apartment on the outskirts of London.

"Thank you, Dexter," Melody said gratefully. She could barely recognise either Dexter or herself. "Could I use the embryos too, please?" She asked. She was nervous about his reply, but thought that it was worth a shot. She was 41, and very aware of her age.

"Okay," he replied immediately. "You can do that, but only if you sign over your share of ownership on this house. I'll give you the equivalent of my wages for three months for a deposit on a London property," he added.

"But that's not fair," Melody said, shocked by his unjustness.

"That's the deal, if you want the embryos," Dexter said. "Oh, and don't take anything out of the house either; it all stays here."

It was very apparent that if Melody was going to have any children from those embryos, she would have to accept this deal. No matter how unkind or unjust this was, she simply needed this opportunity. Those embryos might only be tiny cells at the moment, but to Melody, they were children. They were her children. They were real, alive and waiting for her.

Melody spent the next month frantically looking for an apartment to buy. She also started a job as an assistant to two traders on the Stock Exchange. It was incredibly difficult training for the new job, then after work looking at properties. There was barely time to eat or sleep.

One night, she nearly missed her train stop as she briefly closed her eyes to rest, but fell into a deep sleep instead. She awoke startled and dazed after hearing the name of her train station in a dream. Melody rushed out of the train doors before they shut. Her bag, however, got stuck in-between them. She yanked her bag out of the doors, then make-up, pens, paper and sanitary towels fell across the platform. She held back frustrated tears as she picked everything up. No one helped her; they were all too busy rushing to get home.

Melody got to the house, which no longer felt anything like a home, exhausted. She walked into the kitchen, starving. It was late and she had to get to bed, so she rapidly prepared and ate two slices of toast with honey and an apple. As she sat in the kitchen, Dexter walked in and asked her when she would be leaving.

"I'm trying so hard to find a place as quickly as I can," she said, hating how whiny her voice sounded. She walked towards what was the guest bedroom. "I've only been searching for one month; it took us six months to find this place. It's very difficult to do this by myself."

"Just get out fast," he said slowly. He walked alone into the main bedroom.

Melody collapsed onto her bed in disbelief. She jammed her chair against the door, then lay down. Immediately, she started to cry. She felt immersed in sorrow. The man she believed she would be with forever, whom she loved and thought loved her back had become a monster. She fell asleep in tears, without undressing. When she awoke, her mood was determined.

She put an offer on the first apartment she saw the next day. She took no time to check if it was what she really wanted, but her offer was accepted. Melody figured that it was better to have something and get out than to suffer through this breakup any longer, in his company. Melody stayed away from Dexter; hiding in the guest room when she was at home and staying out of the house as much as possible.

In less than two months, the buying process was finalised and she moved out. She'd never felt relief like she felt when she waved goodbye to the house, and the daffodils that had begun to bloom in the garden.

Chapter Thirty

****

Dexter stepped off the train at Hampstead Heath Station and jostled his way to the exit. He wasn't in a hurry to walk home, so he stopped at the cafe across the road and bought himself a takeaway flat white coffee. Like Melody, he'd been spending a lot of time out of the house. He walked slowly, window-shopping as he went, then caught his reflection in the shop window. He looked at his face. The beard, the darker hair, the adventurous eyes. He was a very different man now, compared to when he first met Melody. He was ready to be free. He couldn't wait until she moved out. Every time he saw her, he felt guilty for breaking up with her and frustrated that she was still there. He needed her gone.

He fantasized about his impending freedom as he walked towards his home. He imagined taking a new girl there. *Maybe I should*, he thought. *Maybe that will get rid of her.*

When he unlocked the front door, he couldn't help but notice that the plant pot near the entrance was gone. As he opened the door, he also noticed that the pictures of sunflowers which had hung in the doorway were gone. Melody had finally moved out. Dexter laughed, then gasped. He'd been unprepared for this to actually happen. Whilst he was incredibly relieved that she'd left, he was surprised by his sudden, overwhelming sadness. Into his mind flashed memories of the fun times they'd had, the love he'd felt for her in the early days, how much she'd helped him.

An era was gone and would never return. He closed the door and allowed his own tears to fall.

Chapter Thirty-One

****

Melody's mobile phone buzzed. She saw his name and allowed her thumb to hover over the 'answer' button. She finally clicked.

"Hello?" she said. She was walking to her apartment in Stratford, with supplies to stock her fridge.

"Hi," said Dexter. "You moved out."

"Yes, I did," said Melody bluntly. "I thought you'd be happy."

"You said you were going at the end of the month," he said. His voice sounded flat and croaky.

"Well, things finalised quicker than I expected. So I thought it would be a good chance to leave earlier," she told him.

"Oh yeah. I guess I was just surprised. I came home to an empty house today and I wasn't expecting that. The next-door neighbours came over and told me you'd moved out. They all felt sorry for me," he said.

Melody could tell he was smiling on the phone. "Well, did you tell them you asked me to move out?" she asked.

"No, of course not!" he replied.

Melody was starting to get angry again. "Thank you for ringing, Dexter, but if you'll excuse me, I have a lot to do. You know, pictures to unpack," Melody told him.

"Yeah, right. Maybe we can still have a coffee together sometime? I don't want to stop our friendship totally," he said.

"Oh, maybe," Melody half-shouted. "At the moment, I think I just need some space, if that's okay. I wish you all the best though. Bye now."

She was seething. She just wanted to tell him where to go and to never, ever contact her again. But, of course, she still felt a little softness and she was very aware of her predicament. She would, after all, need his approval to use their embryos one day.

She shoved her mobile phone into her hand bag and opened the door to her new apartment.

Melody shut the door, placed her bags on the floor and hung her jacket up on the coat hook. She looked around at her new, independent living space. All she had was a few wall pictures, a couple of plants, an inflatable bed, desk and a fridge. The fridge was something the previous owners had thankfully left behind. She didn't yet have chairs or tables, there was no sofa, no proper bed, no washing machine. The room was littered with her suitcases. Her apartment needed a LOT of work. The wallpaper hadn't been removed properly before it had been painted over, so the walls were lumpy, and the windows in their cracked panes needed replacing. To her disgust, there was also mould growing on the walls in the bedroom where the wardrobes had previously been.

She stood in the lounge room and surveyed the walls around her. Although in many ways she was relieved and elated to be there, she couldn't shake her sadness. She reflected on the last 12 months. If someone had told her this time last year she would be living alone, broke in this cramped one-bedroom apartment, she would have laughed at them!

In an attempt to regain control, she opened a notepad from her bag and started to make a list of everything she needed to do and what she had to buy. She was determined to stay positive as she moved forward. She knew that she could put life slowly back together. It would never be the same: it wouldn't be what she'd expected, but it might just end up being better. She had been forced out of her home, but she would survive! Melody knew that what was happening to her was making her stronger. And she had to be strong, to be a mother.

Yes, her plan was to first, sort out her apartment, then, to have the beautiful child she knew she had to have.

Chapter Thirty-Two

****

Over the next two years, Melody renovated her apartment. The feature she was most proud of was the wonderful contemporary gas fire that she had fitted into her lounge room wall, like a picture frame. The fire created a soft and warm ambience. She also kept the place infused with the smell of lavender, which she often burned on her oil burner.

She had some lovely neighbours, but there were a couple she couldn't stand. An Indian man directly next to her played loud Bollywood music every Saturday morning. It drove her mad. She suspected he was on probation, as he was often visited by officials. The neighbour in the apartment below her pained her in a different way. She complained about the sound of her vacuum, and sometimes moaned that she walked around her apartment 'too much'. Melody knew that she didn't walk around 'too much'. Still, she took to wearing fluffy slippers in an attempt to keep the peace.

Every day, she thought about her embryos, but she made up excuses to wait a little bit longer each day. Melody was scared. She was scared to go through IVF, scared of being pregnant and afraid to raise a child by herself. It was easier to wait. She began to tell herself, "Maybe Mr Right might still come along." After many evenings dwelling on that possibility, Melody set upon a mission to find Mr Right. She signed up for internet dating.

Melody met Dominic in Wimbledon for lunch one Saturday. He'd stated on his profile that he was six foot and athletic, but she realised after meeting him, he had elongated his photo. He was much shorter than Melody and had a beer belly. Out of politeness, she suffered through lunch.

"So, what do you think?" he'd loudly asked her, sipping on his glass of Sauvignon Blanc.

"Oh, think about what?" Melody asked.

"About me?" Dominic replied.

Melody was embarrassed by his over-confidence.

"Ah, well, you're very different from your profile," she said, feeling very uncomfortable.

"Yes, but when you get to know me, it won't matter in the end," he said. "Did you know that I own a four-bedroom house just around the corner from here?"

"Is that right?" she answered, adjusting herself in her chair. She looked at the door. Could she run?

"Are you impressed yet?" he asked.

Melody looked up at him. She found it difficult to hide her distaste. "Well, you're a very nice man, but if I'm going to be truthful, I don't think you're right for me," she said. "I am sorry," she added.

Dominic grimaced at her response. "Right then, let's get the bill," he said. "We'll halve it." Then, he downed the rest of his wine.

"But, I only had one main meal, with water. You had two courses, and wine!" Melody said.

"Well, that's what you women get for wanting to be so independent nowadays!" he said.

Melody slammed too much cash on the table and stormed out of the restaurant. She cursed internet dating as she walked to the train station.

Still, she did it again. Melody met Paul in a bar in Clapham Common. After Dominic, she'd vowed never to have a lunch or dinner date again. Paul's profile stated he was an intelligent author and a gym instructor. He did send some rather sexually suggestive texts to her before they met, but she decided to overlook these and meet him anyway.

Obviously, she was disappointed when Paul was a very overweight man, who sweated profusely and had a rather high-pitched voice that shook with nerves.

"Are you a gym instructor, Paul?" Melody asked, looking at his clearly unfit body.

"No, I did that about ten years ago," he replied.

"Oh, okay. Are you currently writing a book?" she asked, trying to sound interested.

"I'm having a little break from writing at the moment," he replied.

"I see. You know, you don't have to feel nervous," she said, trying to put his nerves at ease.

"I can't help it," he said. His voice was getting more and more high-pitched. "My voice changes as well, when I'm nervous," he added. His high-pitched voice was verging on comical. Once again, Melody patiently sat with the man out of politeness, then promptly left after enough time had passed.

Then there was Damon. Melody thought Damon was gorgeous! He was a little taller than her, fit, had a handsome face and a stunning smile. And their personalities fitted together perfectly. He was six years older than her, but didn't look it. They stayed over at each other's apartments and relished long, luscious dinners together, followed by breakfast in bed the next morning. Melody thought everything was going amazingly well and she couldn't believe she'd found someone 'normal' on an internet dating website. However, Damon was newly single after a long-term relationship, and after meeting Melody, he remained a member of the dating website. He openly laughed and bragged about some of the messages he still received from women. Melody, on the other hand, had deleted her profile after she met Damon. It worried her that he was so blatantly communicating with other women.

They were on the train together one Saturday morning, after Damon had stayed at Melody's, when all of her illusions were shattered.

"Hey Mel, my flatmate asked me to go to a Swingers party with him on Saturday," Damon said.

"A what?" asked Melody. She felt a little sick.

"A Swingers party," Damon said. "Do you want to come?" he asked. He was smiling and looked completely casual about the whole thing.

"I don't want to go," Melody said quickly. "That's not my cup of tea."

"Then you won't mind if I go?" he said, remaining upbeat.

"Are you asking me or telling me?" Melody asked. She couldn't hide how annoyed she was.

"Um, well, I'm definitely going," he said.

They hardly spoke for the rest of the train journey, and Melody didn't see him again.

It was after Damon, that Melody finally came to the realisation that she had to be independent. There was no point trying to find the right man in this city of wrong men. Whilst searching, more time had passed and she wasn't getting any younger.

"No more messing around," she told herself firmly.

She was going to have her baby. And she would do it all by herself.

Chapter Thirty-Three

****

Melody brushed her hair, wondering what she'd say to Dexter. It was Saturday morning and she'd planned all week that this would be her time to contact him. The thought of it made her nauseous, but she had to ask for his permission to use their embryos. Her hand trembled as she picked up her mobile phone. They had met up a couple of times for coffee after they had parted, but she hadn't spoken to him for six months.

"Hello," Dexter said as he picked up his phone. His voice sounded deeper than before, and he sounded distracted.

"Hi, it's Melody. Are you okay?" she asked.

"Yeah, not bad," he said, he sounded like his mind was elsewhere. "What's up?" he said.

"Well, I have a pretty important question to ask you. It's about our embryos," Melody said.

"Ah, okay," responded Dexter, slightly hesitating.

"I'd like to contact the IVF clinic to have a child by myself, and the clinic will need your permission for me to use our embryos. Could you help me with that, please?"

Melody's voice was wavering slightly.

"We did have a deal," she added.

There was silence from Dexter. Eventually, he responded. "I'm sorry, but I can't do that."

Melody's heart felt as though it had stopped. "What do you mean?" She said loudly. "We had a deal. I gave you exactly what you wanted," she said.

"Yeah, I know. But if I give you permission, I'll have to pay child maintenance," he said.

"Look, I don't care about that. I just want those embryos, please," Melody said in frustration.

"I'm sorry, but I can't do that," he said again.

"But that's not fair," she shouted. Once again, Dexter was causing tears to fall down her face.

"I'm sorry. I'm not going to give you permission. Goodbye, Melody," Dexter said, then he hung up the phone.

Melody was speechless, angry and frustrated. Not only was she furious about how unfair everything was, Melody also couldn't believe how stupid she'd been to not have this 'deal' written down between the two of them. That whole period had been so turbulent that she hadn't been thinking logically. How could she have trusted him after everything he said and did?

Melody desperately wanted those embryos. She considered the alternatives. She could get pregnant with a donor, or try again to meet someone...

But the more she thought about the alternatives, the more she realised she would never be able to go ahead with any of them. There was no way she could forget those embryos. She couldn't start a life and then just let it freeze until it expired. She couldn't walk away. Melody felt that her baby was there waiting for her, and she couldn't shake off that feeling! But she also felt helpless.

Chapter Thirty-Four

****

Flattening out her skirt, Melody looked at herself in the mirror. She liked her skirt. It had a pretty flowery design and the style complemented her full figure. She put some blusher on her cheeks and lip gloss on her lips. She was getting ready to meet her friend Rosita for coffee. Thoughts of how she could save her embryos came floating back to her again. She just couldn't forget them and had been thinking about them constantly over the last two months. But, she hadn't been able to think of a formidable plan to change Dexter's mind yet.

Her mobile phone rang.

"Hello," she said. She didn't recognise the number.

"Hi, Melody, it's Edmund," the caller said. He sounded rushed and panicky.

"Oh, hi," said Melody, slightly surprised. She was trying to recollect where she'd heard the name Edmund before. Then it dawned on her. Edmund was Dexter's work colleague. She'd met him a couple of times. He'd been drunk on both occasions and she didn't like him. He was arrogant, which she hated and she'd always suspected that he was a bad influence on Dexter.

"Melody, there's been a terrible accident," Edmund blurted out. "Dexter is in hospital. I know you're no longer together, but he's seriously hurt. He's asking for you, he says it's urgent." Edmund exhaled loudly down the phone. "You've got to come here quickly. He's insisting on seeing you."

Melody had never heard Edmund sound like this before. He seemed extremely serious and like he might burst into tears.

"What has happened?" Melody responded directly. She saw in her reflection that she was frowning. She couldn't help but feel concerned for Dexter's welfare.

"I'll fill you in when you arrive. Please come to St Thomas' Hospital as quickly as you can. It's imperative you drop everything and get to Accident and Emergency rapidly," Edmund said. It was clear that he meant it.

"Okay, I'm on my way, Edmund," Melody replied.

"St Thomas' Hospital," Edmund said again. "Be quick!"

"I'm coming now," said Melody, her own voice starting to sound panicky.

She ran from her flat to the closest tube station, then jumped on the next train to Kennington. It took 11 minutes to arrive in Kennington, where she ran up the stairs and onto the street. She flagged down a black cab to take her to St Thomas' Hospital and handed the driver a note. When she arrived, she ran to the Accident and Emergency department and told the receptionist she was there for Dexter. A nurse quickly escorted her to a room filled with beds behind individual curtains. She pointed to the curtain Dexter lay behind and smiled softly.

Melody stood outside Dexter's curtain and took several deep breaths to compose herself. The urgency hadn't left her, but she was terrified of the unknown. She slowly pulled the curtain.

In front of her, lay a completely unrecognisable Dexter. Both his eyes were swollen black and blue and his head was bandaged. His skin looked mottled in colour and his body looked limp. His chest was covered in bandages and it looked as though one of his legs was missing from beneath the bed sheets.

"Oh my God," she gasped, turning to look at the figure who sat on the plastic chair beside the bed.

"What happened?" she asked Edmund. Both his hands were over his face and he was shaking his head. Melody thought that she caught a whiff of alcohol.

"It was an accident!" he said through his hands. It was obvious from his voice that he was crying.

"Dexter stumbled," he said. "He fell in front of a bus. It happened so quickly." Edmund refused to look up at Melody.

"Had you both been drinking?" Melody asked, although she knew the answer.

"Yes, but it was an accident," he said again. "I tried to help him, but it was too late. He's in terrible shape, Melody. He's not long come out of emergency surgery to fix internal bleeding and he's lost part of his right leg."

Melody looked sadly at Dexter. He was unrecognisable. She felt shocked as he grunted her name.

"Melody," he said. "Is that Melody?"

Melody looked at him with her mouth open.

"Dexter?" she said.

"Melody, I'm sorry," said Dexter. His voice was so quiet, Melody had to strain her ears to hear him.

"That's okay, Dexter," she said, suddenly overwhelmed by compassion. "Get some rest."

She looked at his purple face. It was difficult to bear.

"I'm sorry," he said again. "Melody, there's not much time. I want you to have our embryos. I want you to have our child."

Melody couldn't believe what she was hearing.

"Dexter," she said, "get some rest. You're going to be okay. They're taking care of you."

She heard a sniffle from Edmund. Did they know something she didn't?

Melody put her immediate emotions on hold. She knew that she had to capture Dexter's permission.

"Edmund," she said, "please can you film this conversation?"

Edmund looked up at her. She pulled her phone out of her pocket, set it to video and passed it to him.

"Please capture this," she said. "It's incredibly important."

Edmund pointed the phone so that it captured them both. He was confused, but too emotionally exhausted to question it.

"Dexter, can you tell me that again, please?" Melody said clearly. "I need to be sure I heard you correctly."

"Melody, I want you to use our embryos for yourself. I'm so sorry. I want to leave something behind. You would make an amazing mother."

"Thank you, Dexter." Melody couldn't say any more. Tears clouded her eyes as she nodded at Edmund. He stopped the video.

"Is he going to be okay?" she asked Edmund, crying.

Edmund looked at Dexter. He was struggling to breathe or speak now and was plugged into a beeping machine. He had a drip in his arm and his leg; he'd lost half of his leg!

Melody sat on the edge of the bed and took Dexter's hand. She held it with both of her own hands. He managed to squeeze her hand and she softly squeezed it back. It was wet and cold. Slowly, his hand released hers and his eyes glazed over.

"Dexter!" she said, panicking. "Dexter!"

The machines he was connected to started to buzz loudly.

"Dexter!" she shouted, shaking his hand.

Hospital staff poured into the room. They attempted to resuscitate him, but his soul had left his body. He'd accepted his death. In his final moments, Dexter floated at ceiling height, looking down. He saw Edmund stiff with shock, holding his hands over his mouth. He watched Melody's shoulders shake whilst she sobbed with grief behind the doctors who tried to save him.

As Dexter left his body, he didn't feel scared, he felt satisfied. He was content that his life had had purpose. He'd given Melody permission to have his child.

He hoped that she would.

Chapter Thirty-Five

****

Melody felt like she had been hit by lightning. With leaden steps, she walked home from the train station, trying to process what had happened. Visions of Dexter on the hospital bed wouldn't leave her mind. She doubted she would ever forget the disturbing images that would haunt her forever. She shook her head to try and get it out of her mind, but it was no use. She realised that she was still crying.

Melody unlocked her front door and walked to her living room, dropping her handbag on the floor. Then, she sat down at her desk and turned on her laptop. She connected her mobile phone to the device and copied the video of Dexter talking with her tonight. She tried not to look at his face, instead focusing on the message.

"I want you to have our child."

She burnt a DVD of the video and emailed herself a copy.

"This is important," she said to herself.

She closed her laptop and lay on the sofa. She allowed herself to sob, and sob, and sob.

Chapter Thirty-Six

****

Melody watched the funeral proceedings from the back row. She was, after all, Dexter's ex-girlfriend, which made her feel that she didn't quite belong there with his family. She could clearly see Dexter's mother, Roseanne, in her husband, Harold's arms, her shoulders trembling whilst she wept loudly and pitifully.

When the funeral was over and the entourage filed past where Melody was sitting, she then gave her condolences to Roseanne and Harold. It broke her heart to see these two wonderful people overcome with grief. They looked smaller at this time and their eyes were red from days and nights spent crying. They were unable to talk to Melody, but the three of them shared a hug.

******

The funeral was in Auckland, where his family lived. This was also where Melody's embryos were stored. Her head hurt with conflicting emotions, including guilt. She couldn't help but feel excited about (potentially) having a child, but the fact that it was Dexter's death that had led to him giving her permission, tainted the positive emotions. Was she doing the right thing?

After a lot of thinking and a couple more days in Auckland, Melody decided that she was. In a way, having Dexter's child was like helping him to live on and it had been his dying wish. She decided to call the hospital.

Melody was quickly transferred to Monica, the Head Nurse. Her heart was racing as she anticipated the conversation ahead.

"Hi, Monica. I'm hoping you can help me," she said confidently. "I have embryos stored at the hospital and I'm interested in commencing IVF. I would like to know the procedure, please."

Melody inhaled deeply.

"Okay," said Monica, before pausing for what felt like forever. She checked Melody's details, then proceeded with the call.

"I've just checked your information and that's all fine, we'll just need Dexter's consent. It has been quite a while since you froze your embryos. May I ask if you are still in a relationship with Dexter?" she said.

"Well, it is a little complicated, Monica. We were no longer in a relationship, but I do have Dexter's consent to use our embryos by myself," she replied. "Sadly, he gave his consent to me just before he died. I have a video of him doing so."

"Oh, I'm terribly sorry, Melody." Monica was silent for a few seconds.

"I'm sorry," she said again. "Can I please clarify: Were you in a relationship with him when he passed away?"

"No," said Melody, "but I did get permission from him to use the embryos."

Her voice and hands were shaking.

"I see," said Monica, before pausing again. "The only thing is, when you created embryos together, the documents you signed clearly stated at the bottom of the page that if your relationship ended, the embryos would be automatically destroyed. You are only able to use them if you are still in a relationship together," she said.

Melody felt as though she'd been punched in the chest. "But I have Dexter's permission to use them," she said again. "Surely, that counts?"

"I am sorry, but we don't have any guidelines in that situation. We would need to destroy them following the hospital's policies," said Monica.

Although she felt as though she'd received a blow, Melody allowed her strength and determination to return. "But what about these embryos' right to life?" she said. "I want to do the right thing and allow them to live. May I speak with your manager?"

Monica paused again.

"My supervisor, Rebecca, is away on holidays and will be back in two days' time," she said. She sounded tired.

"Okay, please don't do anything with the embryos, Monica. I'll ring back in two days," said Melody.

"Okay," said Monica. "Goodbye."

"Goodbye," said Melody.

As she hung up the phone, she couldn't help but feel deflated. But she had to try; she had to do everything she could to make this happen.

Chapter Thirty-Seven

****

Melody stayed with her long-time and close friend Samantha in Auckland. She was a kind woman, the same age as Melody, who desperately wished she'd had a baby. She looked similar to when they were younger, with perfectly smooth, black hair and bright eyes. They were surrounded by some smile lines now and they still sparkled with happiness from within. She would have been an amazing mother, and it was clear from all her friends who made her godmother to their own children that others thought so as well. But unfortunately, it had never happened to her. When Melody told her all about her fight to save her embryos, Samantha was only too happy to help her. She felt excited and determined on Melody's behalf.

Melody didn't waste any time. She rang the supervisor, Rebecca, on the afternoon she was due to return back from holidays.

"Hi, Rebecca, it's Melody Jefferies. I have some embryos stored at the hospital."

"Hi, Melody. Monica quickly gave me details earlier today as to why you would be ringing," Rebecca said.

"Oh, excellent," said Melody. "About my embryos' right to life."

"You are aware of our policy to destroy embryos after a relationship has ended, right?" said Rebecca.

"Yes, I am," said Melody. "But, I would like to put forward an argument to override that policy, please. I have a video of my ex-partner's permission to use the embryos for myself before he passed away. I believe they are far too valuable to be discarded and what's more, I would make a good mother. I would like to put a case forward, please."

"Okay, well, this is something new. I'm going to have to talk to our head doctor. Are you still in the UK?" Rebecca asked.

"No, I'm here in New Zealand to get permission to use the embryos," Melody said confidently. In reality, her hands were shaking.

"If you can give me your email address and postal address, and I'll be in contact with you after I speak to the doctor. You know, the fact that you have travelled all the way back to New Zealand to pursue this does show how serious you are. That's a good thing, Melody," Rebecca said.

"I can't tell you how much I want those embryos, Rebecca," Melody said, letting her guard down. "I just couldn't imagine them being destroyed."

"I'll see what I can do, Melody," Rebecca said.

Melody gave Rebecca all her details. "Thank you, Rebecca. I look forward very much to hearing from you," she said.

Melody literally crossed her fingers as she said goodbye to Rebecca.

Chapter Thirty-Eight

****

Melody kept herself busy in New Zealand. Instead of sitting and waiting, she set about finding ways to prepare herself to have a child. She was just waiting to receive the good news from the hospital. She applied to study Child Care in a Nursery through an apprenticeship and got accepted. It happened so easily, almost as if it was meant to be.

She spent the evenings with her friend, Samantha and they enjoyed sharing nostalgia together as they reflected on their younger days.

Melody received a letter in the post one afternoon. She could tell from the envelope that it was from the hospital. She sat at the dining table and opened it tentatively. Her heartbeat was rapid, as were her eyes as they scanned the text. The letter informed her that they were considering her request.

"Yes!" Melody shouted. "Yes!"

She read on. The letter stated that she would need to put forward her case in writing and provide evidence of Dexter's permission. The Board of Directors would consider her proposal during their next meeting in two months' time. Behind the letter, was a sheet of paper filled with questions about why they should consider her case.

"Samantha, look at this," Melody said, running to her friend who was reading on the sofa. She handed Samantha the letter. "Look!" She said. Samantha put her book down and took the letter from Melody.

"There is hope. There is still hope!" Melody said loudly.

Samantha read the letter and smiled broadly.

"Melody, this is more than hope! This is a door that is wide open. You get out there and make this happen. Do it for you and also for me. I would have given anything to have this chance." She looked a little sad as her words trailed off.

"I'm going to have a child, Samantha. I can feel it. I can feel it so strongly. I can almost touch that little baby, it feels so real," said Melody.

Samantha hugged her. "I'm so happy for you," she

said. "I'm so happy! This is amazing!"

Melody spent the next week, each night after work, carefully selecting her words. She reflected upon how lucky she was to have started this apprenticeship in the nursery. What a brilliant way to highlight her love for children and to show that she was gaining useful skills to prepare her for becoming a mother. Melody tested a section of her case on Samantha. She sat and listened patiently.

"When I went through IVF with my then partner, I was committed to having a child. These embryos are more than just cells to me. They are the beginning of a life. The end of our romantic relationship didn't alter this feeling one bit. If anything, it became stronger. When Dexter gave me his permission to use our embryos on his death bed, he sounded completely sincere. There was emotion in his voice as he told me he wanted to leave something behind. These embryos are his legacy. It is not the embryos' fault that a relationship ended and their donor passed away. They are little lives, waiting for a loving family, which I can provide them with. I may be a single woman, but I am committed to bringing a child up in the best possible way. I am studying Childcare in a nursery and am doing everything in my power to ensure that I become a loving and knowledgeable mother. I have two strong arms that welcome the love of a child and a donor who has given me permission. Please help me to fulfil my dream, to give love and care to a child. I promise to be the best mother I can be."

"Well, something like that," Melody said and smiled at Samantha.

"Oh, that was so sincere, and I could feel it was coming directly from your heart. I hope they vote for you, Melody, and I'm going to pray for you tonight," Samantha said softly.

"Thank you. It'll be a very long wait until the next board meeting. I don't know if I'll be able to sleep!" Melody said. Her heart beat rapidly again.

Chapter Thirty-Nine

****

Dr White waited in line at the hospital kiosk. He was early for the board meeting, as he felt especially interested. He remembered Dexter and Melody from all those years ago. Dexter was a young, good-looking man, and Melody a gentle and kind lady who desperately wanted to have children. He remembered them because they wanted to freeze their embryos and put motherhood on hold for Melody. That wasn't a normal request back then, and he secretly thought they wouldn't be having any children. However, when he heard from Rebecca about their breakup and of Dexter's passing, he felt connected to Melody's struggle to have a child.

He hoped she'd win, but there were those on the board who didn't want to break the rules, and didn't feel it was a struggle worth fighting for. Dr White ordered a cappuccino, then marched with it to the meeting room.

There were 13 attendees, including the board of directors, IVF professional doctors and the chairperson. They were all highly professional and esteemed individuals who were well-versed in the hospital system. They promptly talked through each item on the agenda, until finally, Melody's request was to be voted on. The chairperson, Dr Tulley, who was a large gruff and authoritarian figure, announced the topic.

"Melody versus the Hospital," he said dismissively. "Melody had IVF with her partner and they froze their embryos. Their relationship ended and her ex-partner passed away. She would now like to use her embryos as a single woman. She received consent to do so from her ex-partner before he died. Should the hospital allow this? The hospital's policy is currently to destroy all embryos from couples whose relationships have dissolved."

Dr Ryan, a short man with a receding hair line and a large belly, immediately spoke, "I think we shouldn't even delve into this. It's better to have a blanket rule with regards to this policy. I think it will complicate matters too much". He was one of the members of the board of directors.

Dr Tulley frowned at him and interrupted. "Melody has sent in a video of her ex-partner giving his permission. I'm going to show this now before we proceed further."

He used the remote control to automatically roll the projection screen down into place. He connected his laptop wirelessly to the projector and started the video. The board watched in silence as the emotion of the video pierced every corner of the room. After it had ended, no one spoke for more than a minute. Throats were cleared, glasses of water were filled and sips were taken. This video had clearly touched all of the occupants in the room and each board member tried their best to hold onto their composure.

Dr Bodem, one of the only females in the room, was the first to speak. "Every embryo should be given a right to life, as Melody has pointed out in her statement." She also added, "She clearly is a positive woman who has set her objectives. She is studying childcare in readiness to be a mother. Someone who so ambitiously wants to be a mother should be allowed that right. After watching this video, I can see no hesitation in letting her use the embryos."

Dr Bodem exuded a professional air about her that demanded respect. As she spoke, the majority of the men in the room found themselves nodding.

"I tend to mostly agree," added Dr Bridge, a board member in his late sixties. "But, my concern is, was Dexter of sound mind when he gave her his permission?"

Dr Addleson, another director added, "It is clear to me, especially due to Dexter's mottled skin, that he was in his last moments before death. No doubt he would have been on pain killers as well. However, his words were coherent. His speech is slow, but direct and he was able to get his point across to Melody. No one is encouraging him to speak or are putting words in his mouth. His words are of his own and they are emotionally charged. I believe this video should be counted." Dr Addleson was one of the younger members of the board, but was well respected for his work.

"I remember this couple," said Dr White, prompting surprised glances in his direction. "I would give a yes vote to Melody. But I would feel more comfortable if she has IVF in another clinic for future treatment."

Dr Ryan grunted loudly.

"This is a complicated story," Dr White continued, "But I think I know just the clinic. Dr Thompson is the Director at the Green Lodge Clinic. She would be sympathetic to Melody's plight."

Dr Addleson spoke up again, "We would need to have our legal team involved to write up the paperwork giving her full ownership, so we get this right the first time. This is an unusual situation, but that doesn't mean it won't happen again."

Dr Ryan butted in, "I still think this is a bad idea."

"Okay, let's put this to vote, everyone," said the chairman. "Melody will be allowed to have full access to her embryos and our legal team will organise the correct paperwork confirming this. Dr White will approach Dr Thompson in the Green Lodge Clinic, to see if it is possible to transfer Melody's embryos over there for her to have future treatment. All in favour?" asked the chairman.

Nine hands raised in favour.

"All those opposed?" asked the chairman.

Four hands were raised.

"I hereby announce this item as passed and approved," said the chairman.

Dr White smiled.

Chapter Forty

****

Melody ran up the hill in the play ground singing 'The Grand Old Duke of York' with two giggling four-year-old girls. They were Willow and Virginia. They both had blonde hair and cheeky smiles, but Willow seemed extra-special to Melody. She was such a fun little girl with a wonderful, sensitive side to her that shone through. Melody couldn't help but imagine she was her own, sometimes. The children ran down the other side of the hill and pretended to fall over, rolling all over the ground, laughing loudly. Melody looked at her watch. It was after 3 pm and the parents would be here soon. She started to gather the children to take them to the school building.

The nursery leader, Mrs Patal, asked everyone to sit down as she led the children to sing their 'farewell' song. Parents were lining up outside the door and they soon filtered in to collect their children. Willow came over to Melody and gave her a loving hug as she was leaving.

"Bye-bye, Melody, see you tomorrow," Willow said cheerily.

"Bye-bye, Willow," said Melody, feeling touched.

She thought to herself, *If I'm so lucky to have a little girl one day, I'm going to call her Willow.* Melody smiled hopefully to herself as she dreamt of holding a little baby. She held that thought in her mind as she tidied up the classroom, humming with a soft smile on her lips. She hummed all the way to Samantha's home on the bus. When she arrived, she habitually opened the mailbox. There was an official-looking letter on the bottom, with her name on it. Melody turned it over and she spied the hospital address on the back. She tore it open and quickly scanned the contents. Her eyes widened. She beamed for a while, then started jumping up and down with excitement. She waved the letter in the air and shouted, "Yes!"

Chapter Forty-One

****

Melody was euphoric. The hospital letter stated that the embryos were now 100% hers and they had been transferred to another clinic in Auckland. The Green Lodge Clinic. She could go there and begin the process. She could get pregnant. She was going to do it!

As she caught her breath from the excitement, anxiety struck her. Was she ready? Where would she bring up a child? Could she afford it? When should she go ahead with IVF? So many questions buzzed around her head.

Melody was in the last stages of her Childcare Apprenticeship and had been told that she could receive her certificate six months early. It usually took at least one year to complete her studies, but she'd bulldozed through the curriculum. She had learnt much about babies and caring for young children, which had really built her confidence about being a mother. She did, however, have reservations about her finances. Melody decided to return to London to make and save more money to prepare for her baby. She'd loved every moment of working in childcare and would miss her time with the children in New Zealand, especially Willow. But having a baby right at this moment scared her. She needed some savings.

With this in mind, Melody made plans to return to London.

Chapter Forty-Two

****

Melody settled back into work at her old job. It was good to be back and into her old routine after such an emotional few months. She collected some savings as the months whizzed by. It was ten months into her return that a trip to the doctor shook her up. She went to see her GP, Dr Murphy, to get some antibiotics for a chest infection. Dr Murphy was a similar age to Melody, but she looked a little older. Her dark, wavy hair was speckled with grey and her glasses made her look wise. Melody liked her doctor, and had told her all about the embryos. After she'd written the prescription, Dr Murphy stopped and looked solemnly at Melody.

"Melody, tell me, what is happening with your embryos now?" she said. "I thought you may be having IVF soon?"

"Oh, yes, I want to. It's just, I don't know if I'm fully ready yet," replied Melody, smiling.

"How old are you now?" asked Dr Murphy, still looking solemn.

"I'm 44," Melody said.

Dr Murphy nodded. "You know, you look good for your age, but your womb is 44 years old." She paused. "It may seem harsh for me to say this to you, but if you don't do this now, you may never have children. You could miss the chance. Don't leave it too late, Melody."

Melody felt a lump in her throat. Her eyes started to well, and the tear gates opened. Dr Murphy put her hand on her shoulder as she cried.

"I'm scared," Melody said. "I don't know if I can do this by myself. I don't know if I'm financially ready."

Dr Murphy passed her a tissue, then looked her in the eye. "You can do this; you are in a much better position than a lot of people who already have children. You'll be okay. You'll see."

Melody couldn't say anything; she was still trying to contain her tears. She nodded appreciatively at Dr Murphy, blew her nose embarrassingly loudly and gathered her things. She walked away from the surgery rekindling her hopes and dreams. She needed to do this. She needed to do what she'd always wanted to do. Now.

When she got home, Melody sent an email to the IVF clinic stating that she wanted to start IVF. She booked a flight to New Zealand. As she lay down in bed, still ill with the chest infection, she felt content. Melody knew she needed to get better quickly. She needed to go to work, so that she could apply for yet more time off.

She fell into a light sleep, comforting herself that this was it. This was finally it.

Chapter Forty-Three

****

After that day, everything happened incredibly quickly. Melody boarded a plane at Heathrow and headed to Auckland with every intention of collecting her little baby. She stayed with Samantha again, and as soon as she dropped her suitcases in Samantha's spare bedroom, Melody made an appointment at the Green Lodge Clinic. She did not want to waste any more time. She felt blessed when she was slotted into a cancelled appointment for the following day.

******

Melody opened the clinic door and introduced herself to the receptionist. She was a petite, mature woman with incredibly long fingernails. Melody wondered how she managed to type with those nails. It seemed impossible. She pondered on this as she sat in the waiting area. She was surrounded by hopeful couples, nervously waiting to start their own IVF adventures. Everyone except for Melody was part of a couple. Many were snuggled up and holding hands. She felt isolated.

It was like she had arrived on a couples-only island, and at the last minute her partner had deserted her. Nobody looked at her, but she still felt self-conscious.

"Melody," announced the nurse.

She stood up and avoided looking anywhere except for the direction the nurse led her in. They walked into a room that felt like a lounge room, minus the TV.

"The director of our clinic, Dr Thompson, will be in to see you soon. Please take a seat," the nurse told her.

Melody felt nervous. Recollections of her fight for her embryos suddenly surfaced. The realisation that she was incredibly lucky to be given this chance was on her mind. Something told her that Dr Thompson was a key player in making this happen. At that moment, the door opened, and in strode a smartly dressed lady with short blonde hair. She had an air of confidence that radiated from within. She sat down next to Melody and turned diagonally to face her and smiled. "I'm so glad to finally meet you, Melody," she said.

"It's lovely to meet you too, Dr Thompson," Melody replied.

"How are you feeling? Do you feel ready to give

IVF a go?" Dr Thompson said, smiling.

"I've waited such a long time and I'm ready," replied Melody. "Thank you so much for letting me undergo my IVF treatment at your clinic, Dr Thompson. Thank you, from the bottom of my heart," she said.

Dr Thompson could feel the sincerity of each heartfelt word from Melody and could feel the emotion that oozed from her. Her face softened. "You're so welcome, Melody. I wish you all the luck in the world. I sincerely hope you will have your baby," Dr Thompson said. It was evident that she too was being sincere.

Dr Thompson filled in a couple of forms in silence, then looked up at Melody. "The nurse will give you advice on your medication. Please follow all her instructions and we'll see you back here in one month." She warmly smiled at Melody and stood up. A nurse entered and Doctor Thompson turned to leave the room.

"Goodbye, Melody," she said. "And good luck!"

"Thank you," Melody said, feeling humbled. Dr Thompson left the room and a smiling nurse took her seat.

Bring on the medication, Melody thought. *Let's get this womb ready!*

Chapter Forty-Four

****

Melody was given multiple tablets, nasal spray, instructions and a to-the-day plan for the next few weeks. This was a crucial time to prepare her body to accept an embryo. She felt the urge to be around children as well, so Melody asked if she could stay with her special friend, Indira, or Indy as she liked to be called. She had known Indy for many years, from when they used to be travel agents together, and they'd also been on several joint holidays together. Indy was married with three children, now aged three, five and seven.

Staying with Indy was the perfect stopover before collecting a very precious package. Indy lived in Hatfields Beach, north of Auckland. It was the perfect place to raise children to love the outdoors, with its expansive beach, rocky areas and inlet. Indy's three children had all learnt to swim at a young age, and they loved to kayak, play for hours on the beach and go rock pooling as a family. Indy was delighted to have Melody stay with her. She welcomed her into their impressive five-bedroom home which overlooked the beach. The house was built to capture the scenic beach views which were right on their doorstep. It had been designed by her husband, Henry, who was an architect. Their lounge room view of the beach was magnificent and remained equally stunning at night, especially during a full moon. Indy enjoyed chatting with Melody about the old days when they were young and single. The children loved Melody, and she played with them effortlessly. Melody's staying made Indy realise how much she missed her.

"We have so much to catch up on, Melody!" she said, as they sat on her garden chairs with a bottle of wine. "I was so sorry to hear about Dexter."

"Oh, Indy," Melody said, feeling warm with love for her friend. "Dexter completely broke my heart, and it was so difficult watching him die. I still see images of how he looked on the hospital bed. I know I'll never forget how he looked that day," Her voice cracked with emotion.

"Oh no, that's awful. I'm so sorry," said Indy, "I know how much you loved him once."

"Life is so unpredictable," replied Melody, "If

Dexter hadn't died, he would never have given me permission to use our embryos. You know, I realise now, that I expected too much from him at his age when we were together. He was, after all, eleven years younger than me," she paused. "I always used to say, 'love conquers all', but it's just not true."

Indy shook her head sorrowfully, then touched Melody's arm gently.

"I'm sure that 'love could conquer all', with the right person," she said.

"I can't help but be a little bit jealous of you and Henry," said Melody. "You're so lucky, Indy. It's impossible to find a man now at my age."

Indy shook her head. "Love does come in many shapes and forms, though, Melody. I'm so proud of what you have achieved. You haven't just waved goodbye to those embryos and moved on. Damn it! You're so gutsy and bold to do this all on your own," she said, emphasising her words with her hands. "I don't think I could do it," she added.

"Thank you," said Melody. "I know I couldn't have gone through life without trying. I hope I can bring a little child to life from my embryos. I really do."

"I have a feeling you will, Melody," Indy said. She gave her friend a warm hug.

******

Indy was a stunning lady. She was of slim build and fair skin with a spattering of freckles. She had a heart-shaped face framed with thick red hair, which she straightened daily. Melody had never met anyone with a heart-shaped face before. It made Indy seem unique and mystical. Her children were also quite individual-looking. Mathilda, who was seven years old, had brunette hair, a cheeky smile and an outgoing personality. Isabelle, who was five, had red hair and was curious and petite. Brody, who was three years old, was a slight young boy with strawberry blond hair and a sensitive personality. Their personalities were as individual as their looks. Melody loved looking after the three of them. Their pet dog, Barley, was an irreplaceable part of the crew as well.

One morning, Melody awoke and rolled over. Mathilda was lying there next to her, staring at her face. Melody jumped with surprise.

Mathilda giggled loudly.

"Oh my goodness. Mathilda, you scared me! You crazy girl!" said Melody, laughing with her.

"Sorry. I've been waiting for you to wake up. Sleepyhead!" said Mathilda. "It's the weekend. Will you take us to the beach?" she asked.

Melody stretched and yawned. "Sure, should we walk? We can take Barley then," she said.

"Yeah, let's do it," Mathilda said, bouncing on the bed.

"Want to race down to the kitchen to see your mum?" asked Melody, sitting up. Mathilda was already running down the stairs, laughing and giggling as she went.

Melody spent the next few weeks at Indy's home, playing with the children, walking Barley along the beach and also sitting and meditating for hours on the beach. This was her antidote, and it was just what she needed. She connected with her body during those meditative hours, and let her mind wander. She imagined holding her own baby. She could almost smell the baby smell, almost touch its soft hair and hear its little baby chatter. She connected with her womb and focussed on making that part of her body healthy and fruitful. She followed her pre-IVF instructions religiously. There was no better place to be than close to the beach, with Indy and her family, to emotionally and physically prepare herself to receive her embryo.

Every day, Melody had to take some kind of medication, and for a time, nasal sprays as well. She very carefully documented exactly what she took each day. She was not leaving anything to chance. She was just getting used to the routine, when the moment to return to the IVF clinic in Auckland to collect her embryo arrived. Melody packed her hire car ready for her journey and prepared to leave.

"Don't go!" said Mathilda with tears in her eyes. She grabbed onto Melody's leg and held her still.

"Oh, I've had an amazing time with you three gorgeous children," Melody said, lifting Mathilda off her and drawing her into a hug. "Look after your mum," she said with a heavy heart. She then hugged Isabelle and Brody. She would miss this loving family.

"Thank you for letting me stay, Indy," she said. "You've helped me so much and I've loved staying with you. I've loved every bit of chaos!" she laughed.

"The chaos was the best!" Indy giggled, as the children laughed along beside them. "I wish you so much luck, Melody, and go and get your baby!" she said quietly.

They shared a long, sincere hug before Melody stepped into the car.

Chapter Forty-Five

****

Melody travelled from Samantha's to Green Lodge Clinic on the bus. She felt sick with anxiety. *Relax, Melody, relax,* she kept telling herself. *The more relaxed I am, the better the outcome will be.*

She arrived at the clinic one and a half hours early. She felt ridiculous turning up that early, so she stopped at the door and spun around. Melody wondered what to do to pass some time. She decided to try to trick herself into thinking it was just another day. She would go grocery shopping.

Looking up and down the aisles, she shopped for healthy post-embryo transferral food. Her grocery trolley was full of fresh fruit and vegetables, fish, eggs, whole grains, and of course, there were a couple of chocolate blocks as well. This embryo would have to get used to chocolate; it was a supplement as far as Melody was concerned.

Melody walked back to the clinic again, this time only fifteen minutes early; however, she was now holding onto four large shopping bags. It had seemed a good idea to go shopping, but now she felt silly again. She gently pushed the door open with her foot and tried to manipulate her shopping bags through the door. It wasn't that easy, and they were making such a rustling racket, disturbing the silence of the clinic. She checked in at the reception and sat in the waiting room, surrounded by her bags. Once again, she was surrounded by couples. One of the couples seemed to be staring at Melody's shopping. One by one, they were invited into the clinic room.

"Melody," announced the scientist.

She picked up her shopping and walked towards the woman.

"I see you've been busy," the scientist said. Her name was Lucy, she was Chinese and had a natural, warm smile.

"Ah, yes," replied Melody. "I thought I'd pretend today was a normal day," she replied. She was very embarrassed about bringing her shopping in now.

"Got any eggs in there?" asked Lucy, laughing.

"Oh yes, about half a dozen and of very fine

quality." Melody laughed.

Lucy directed her to sit down as they both laughed and she showed Melody her embryo that would be implanted that day. It was a black and white photo, magnified so Melody could see it clearly. It looked perfect! This was the one. As Melody's embryos had been frozen for six whole years, only one had survived the thawing process. It felt like a miracle.

"I feel quite sure this is a strong embryo, Melody," Lucy assured her. "It's continuing to multiply as we speak."

"It looks just perfect," Melody said.

Taking her picture back to her seat in the waiting room, Melody kept staring at her embryo. She was completely in awe. What a resilient embryo! It had been frozen for six years, defrosted and now was growing into a little baby. She loved it already! After a while, her name was called out again. Melody's heart skipped a beat and her legs felt weak. She really wished she hadn't brought in this shopping now. The nurse took her to a small room and she sat on the end of the clinical bed as she waited for the doctor. Melody was nervous and the nurse attempted to make conversation.

"Are you feeling okay, Melody?" the nurse asked her. "My name is Sarah."

"Yes, I think so," replied Melody. "I'm feeling incredibly nervous though," she added.

"That's perfectly normal," Sarah said. "Everyone feels like that. I see you've been shopping." Sarah smiled, waving at Melody's groceries.

"Yes, that was my attempt to keep everything as normal as possible today." Melody laughed. The amount of reactions told her that patients didn't often take groceries to their appointments.

Just then the door opened and the doctor walked in. He had a friendly, kind and sincere face. He must have been in his mid-fifties.

"Hi, Melody, I'm Dr Marly. Are you ready?" he asked.

Suddenly, Melody burst into tears. She hadn't felt them coming. She definitely felt nervous, but was completely unprepared for the influx of emotions she was feeling right now.

Dr Marly and Sarah exchanged glances. Sarah passed the tissue box to Melody, and Dr Marly looked worried. "Have you changed your mind? You don't have to do this today, if you don't feel ready," he said.

"No, no, I definitely want to go ahead. It's just that all the medication I've been taking is making me feel emotional. I've waited years for this day, and I'm more than ready. Please do go ahead," Melody firmly told Dr Marly, blinking back her tears.

Dr Marly asked for the scientist to come in. Lucy very slowly and carefully walked in, carrying a small wooden rectangular box. She placed it on the side table. Dr Marly very carefully took off the lid. Inside was a see-through oblong thick-looking needle with a blunt end. It was filled with liquid, and there were two air bubbles, one at each end.

"Why are there air bubbles?" Melody asked.

"That's so I know exactly where the embryo is. It's between the two bubbles," Dr Marly said.

Sarah asked Melody to lie down on the bed and placed a sheet over the lower half of her body. She was aware of some activity which was just slightly uncomfortable. Hardly any time seemed to have passed at all when Dr Marly stood up and placed the needle on the table.

"All done," he said. "That wasn't so bad, was it?"

"Wow," said Melody, relieved and excited, "That's it? Really? Easy peasy!"

She sat up slightly. "Is it safe inside there now? I mean, can I walk, you know normally?" she asked.

"Yes, of course," Dr Marly replied with a smile.

"It's just like a jam sandwich in there," added Sarah, the nurse.

Melody laughed at the bizarre analogy.

******

Sitting on the bus on the way to Samantha's home, still surrounded by shopping bags, Melody thought about the tiny, strong embryo inside her now. She felt excited and anxious. Was it growing? What was happening right now? Was this it? Was she a mother?

Chapter Forty-Six

****

With her micro-cargo tucked away in her womb, it was time to go back home to London. As Melody settled in her seat in the plane, she put her hands on her tummy. She felt protective of that area now, and definitely in her mind, she felt pregnant. Even if this pregnancy was not to last, no one was going to take away that feeling.

She watched the clouds out of the plane window and felt that she was floating in them. Life had never felt so wonderful.

As they flew, Melody felt suddenly close to God in the sky. She closed her eyes and sent out a request.

Dear God, please, may all be well in my womb and may this beautiful little embryo flourish. May this embryo stay right here in my tummy, and may I experience a joyous and healthy pregnancy.

Amen.

She crossed her fingers and toes.

Chapter Forty-Seven

****

When Melody got back to London, she immediately returned to work. She felt incredibly lucky to have an employer who allowed her to have so much time off. She didn't get paid during her time off, but the trip was worth it to collect her precious little package. With her embryo inside her, she felt great. There was nothing anyone could do to dampen her spirits.

Melody strode into work. Her role as a corporate receptionist was perfect whilst she was trying to have a baby. It was significantly less stressful than her previous working positions. Her previous jobs had involved managing a project renovating a Chelsea apartment, working in a stressful environment assisting traders at the Stock Exchange and she had also been a personal assistant to a high-profile businessman organising his private jet. Now she booked limousines and meetings for investment businessmen. It was a breeze.

"Good morning," she said to the security guard as she walked through the door.

"Good morning, Melody," replied Samuel. "You sure seem happy! Have you found yourself a boyfriend?" he asked.

"If I do find one, you'll be the first to know!" Melody laughed back at him. "I'm just feeling good!" She smiled.

Melody loved feeling pregnant. Knowing there was a little life growing inside her made her feel complete. Her energy levels were high, and she already felt a nurturing love for this newly forming child.

Melody awoke on Saturday morning feeling happy and enthusiastic. Monday was her first scan, at six weeks, and she was looking forward to it. The neighbour played his loud Bollywood music, and she pulled herself out of bed. She would have to do something about that loud music soon. It was absurd. After pouring bran flakes into her cereal bowl, she bent down to get some milk out of the fridge. She felt a strange sensation in her tummy and instantly straightened up. Something didn't feel right. She felt a strong cramp, followed by another more painful one and wetness between her legs.

"Oh God, no, no, no, no, no!" Melody stammered. She ran to the bathroom and discovered, to her horror, she was bleeding.

"Oh no, no, no, no, no, no, no, no," was all she could say. She felt a rush of sadness and all-consuming disbelief. *This can't be happening!*

Another cramp. What should she do? Should she go to hospital? Melody decided she would probably end up in a waiting room for hours before anyone would attend to her anyway, so she decided to stay at home. What could they do if she went in? Her instinct told her to stay at home and trust in her body. She gathered some towels, laid them in the middle of her bed, propped up her legs, laid down and prayed. Melody had always been close to God and believed she was a part of the entire universe in some small way. She felt that every religion should be revered and respected and there was a place for everyone. She desperately needed some help, and she spoke to God from her heart that day. Melody could have telephoned a friend, but she would have received sympathy. She didn't want anyone's sympathy; she wanted to send out her heart to the universe and ask it to please let her have this child.

She spoke out loud. "Please, God, could You help me to be a mother? Please, please, please. Could You send me Your strength and help my little embryo? I need You to help me and stop this miscarriage."

Wave after wave of cramps and blood loss. Melody only got out of bed to get chocolate from the kitchen and go to the bathroom. Each time she went to the bathroom she felt distressed, but she tried her best to stay calm.

It was late afternoon now. Melody prayed again, "Dear God, thank You for helping me so far to become a mother. Please, I wish to still be pregnant. I promise solemnly to You that I will try to be the best mother I can be." She said this out loud with hands clenched, eyes closed and her head tilted towards the sky. This was the most spiritual she had ever felt in her life. She felt connected to the cycle of life.

Gradually, the cramps stopped. She lay still in bed, not daring to move. Eventually, she got up and cleaned herself up. She had no idea if she had lost her baby or not. Feeling empty and sad after her ordeal, she stayed in her apartment. She didn't have the energy to answer any phone calls or text messages. She felt weak. Sunday slowly came around and Melody quietly waited for her appointment on Monday. She was scared to think she had lost her baby. It was too painful to consider. Monday slowly ticked over. Melody quietly dressed and prepared herself for her appointment. She tried to stay calm and not think too much about the potential sad news that may lie ahead of her today. She walked to the bus stop in a solemn, but quietly purposeful way. She crossed her fingers, and with all her will wished she was still pregnant. She tilted her head up to the blue sky and let the sunshine warm her face. Could she still be pregnant?

Half an hour later, Melody sat in the reception area of the ultrasound clinic. Although her heart felt contracted, she still held onto a glimmer of hope. Ruth, the ultrasound technician, called her into the clinic room.

"Hi, Melody, how are you?" she asked.

"Hi, actually, I'm not feeling so good. I think I had a miscarriage on Saturday," Melody said, fighting to hold back her tears.

"Oh," Ruth said, looking taken aback by the response. "Can you tell me about your symptoms, please?"

Melody described the blood loss and the cramping to Ruth.

"Did you go to hospital?" Ruth asked.

"I probably should have, but instead I lay in bed and prayed," Melody replied.

"Oh, Melody, I'm so sorry to hear this. It does sound like you had a miscarriage. But let's take a look, shall we? Now, don't worry, if I don't say anything for a while. It may be hard to spot, okay?" Ruth explained.

"Okay," replied Melody as she lay down on the examination table.

Ruth rolled the ultrasound device over Melody's belly after applying some extremely cold gel first. The room was eerily silent for five minutes. Melody held her breath, crossed her fingers and waited.

And waited... It felt longer than five minutes.

"I can see a heartbeat!" Ruth announced. "Look!" There on the screen was a tiny half-moon shape with a strong heartbeat.

Melody started to cry with relief. She didn't say anything for a while. Quiet tears streaked her face as she stared at the screen. "It's so small, Ruth," she finally said.

"Your baby is the size of a sesame seed right now," she explained. "After what you just told me earlier, I'm so surprised and happy for you, Melody," Ruth added.

"I can't believe it!" Melody elatedly replied. "I'm pregnant! I'm pregnant!" she repeated. Melody would never forget that day. Her sesame seed-sized baby held on tight to its mummy! It fought to stay right there and won!

Her heart beamed with love and pride.

Chapter Forty-Eight

****

Melody's pregnancy was full of love, happiness and joy. Every second that she was pregnant felt blissful. She welcomed every stage with open arms, even the difficult and more challenging parts. During her early pregnancy, she managed to keep her morning sickness confined to home, not taking one day off work during that time period. One morning, Melody had to rush out the door and was just about to lock it when she felt the contents of her stomach begin to rise. She dashed quickly back inside, vomited into the toilet, brushed her teeth, had a drink of water, then left the apartment again. Then, she smiled all the way as she walked to the train station. She wasn't upset by the sickness at all, as it was proof that she was still pregnant. She felt overwhelmed with love.

******

It wasn't long before the time came for another check-up at the hospital. Melody sat patiently in the waiting area, her hands wrapped around her belly. The midwife called her name and she was escorted to the small clinical room. Melody liked this midwife. Her name was Lola and she was originally from Nigeria. Lola was always jovial and Melody was pleased to see her. As she sat down in the clinical room, Lola commented, "Oh my goodness, look at you, Melody. You are in a real bubble of love, aren't you? You look radiant."

"I'm absolutely loving being pregnant," Melody replied. She loved her maternity appointments, as she was able to listen to her baby's heartbeat. Melody felt closer to her child than ever before when she was able to listen to the rhythm of its life.

Before it was even born, she connected strongly with her baby. She became increasingly content as each day passed.

Chapter Forty-Nine

****

Melody's friend, Grace, waited for her at a window table in their favourite coffee shop. The area was well-lit, and although the sun wasn't shining today, the table was immersed in natural light. It added a shine to her auburn hair, which flowed to the middle of her back and complemented her warm, brown eyes. She was smartly dressed in a blazer and long skirt, and she looked confident and professional as she sat, waiting to be served. She flagged down Melody as she walked into the cafe. "Over here, Melody." Melody walked straight over, and they smiled and hugged each other.

The cafe was not far from Waterloo Station. They both ordered an Italian hot chocolate – the kind you can stand your spoon upright in. It was a delicious treat.

"How was your holiday with your family, Grace?" Melody asked.

"It was good fun! We love those holidays, inclusive of all you can eat and drink. Uncle Bill got so drunk one night, he entertained everyone moonwalking all over the dance floor. It was hilarious! At least he stayed upright this time!" Grace said, laughing.

Grace didn't have a boyfriend or any children of her own, but her family were close knit, and they all managed a yearly family holiday together. All her uncles, aunts, cousins, nieces, nephews and her parents would go away together, and she always brought back a funny story when she returned. It was nearly always about Uncle Bill.

"Poor Uncle Bill! I wonder what he will do next time." Melody laughed. "Hey, I've got some news to share with you," she said. She'd been dying to tell her since before she walked through the door.

"Really? What is it?" said Grace, frowning slightly.

"I'm pregnant!" Melody blurted out.

The waiter brought their drinks over and smiled at them both.

"Oh my gosh! Wow! That is such amazing news!" said Grace. She nodded to thank the waiter, then jumped out of her seat and hugged Melody. "You did it!" she said loudly. "I'm just so happy for you, Melody," she said. Tears of joy formed in her eyes.

"Thank you," said Melody, wiping away a tear of joy herself. "I can't believe it's happening now. It feels like a dream."

"I get first dibs on babysitting, okay?" Grace asked, pushing the spoon into her chocolate.

"You got it! First dibs to you." Melody laughed.

"Seriously though, I can't wait to go on this journey with you. Please ask me if you ever need any help," Grace said.

"Thank you. I'm so excited," said Melody.

Grace's love and support was part of a larger network of friends who were showering Melody with affection and offers of help. Nothing could bring her mood down.

Melody told her boss, who thankfully was supportive, although when people at work found out, there was some speculation as to how she got pregnant, though. Melody heard a rumour that she'd apparently had an affair with a married man. She just laughed. The security guard she worked with joked, "You should have said 'no' a few months ago!" But Melody held her chin up high and smiled contentedly.

She had nothing to be ashamed about. She knew how lucky she was.

Chapter Fifty

****

Grace met Melody outside the hospital. "You look wonderful, Melody! Look at your bump!" she said, pointing at a visibly pregnant stomach.

Melody put her arms around her belly, pulling her dress over her bump to make it stand out. "I know, we're getting bigger," she said.

"You are going to be like an orange," said Grace.

Melody laughed at the idea. "Let's go! I'm dying to find out what I'm having. I swear, this is the most exciting day of my life, other than actually finding out I was pregnant," Melody said.

Melody and Grace took the elevator to the hospital ultrasound clinic, which was on the third floor, and sat down in the waiting room to be called. They flicked through the pages of the magazines on offer from the coffee table while they waited. After twenty minutes, Melody's name was announced, and Grace and Melody went into the clinical room. Ruth, from the ultrasound clinic, was sitting behind a desk, typing on the computer and waiting.

"Hi, Ruth! What a surprise," said Melody. "You work here too."

"Hi, Melody! I thought I recognised your name. Yes, I work in different private practises and this hospital. It's good to see you again. You look radiant!" Ruth said, smiling.

Melody enjoyed hearing that. "Thank you," she said. "This is my friend Grace. She's giving me some moral support today."

Ruth smiled at Grace.

"Let's see how your baby is getting on, shall we?" she said, gesturing at the bed. "Pop up here on the bed and we'll take a look."

Melody lay down on the clinic bed. Ruth looked at her baby with the ultrasound device. Melody could see her baby clearly on the monitor. She saw little hands and feet, and her baby's side profile. Instantly, she found her baby amazing. Ruth spent several minutes taking different measurements of her baby and tapping data into the computer.

"Your baby looks normal and healthy, Melody," she said eventually, then, the question Melody had been waiting for, "Would you like to know if you're having a boy or a girl?"

"Yes, please," said Melody. She held her breath.

"Okay then. You are going to have a little girl," Ruth told her, smiling.

Melody couldn't even speak.

"That is fabulous, Melody!" Grace said.

At that moment, the little girl on the monitor started moving her hand. "Look, she's waving at you!" said Grace, her eyes glowing with amazement.

"She really does look like she's waving, doesn't she?" said Melody. She blinked back tears of joy. She was purely, blissfully happy. There could only be one name for this gorgeous little girl, 'Willow'.

As Melody's tummy continued to grow, so did Melody's love for Willow. Each night, Melody sang Willow a lullaby before falling asleep. She felt as though a love bubble was enveloping the two of them.

Melody was already in love with her gorgeous little girl.

Chapter Fifty-One

****

There was just one downside to Melody's pregnancy. It made her clumsy.

She was well into the third trimester of her pregnancy when she was asked to cover at a different reception for the day. She was waiting by the elevator at work, to go to the cafe on the third floor, when her phone beeped. Annisa had texted her. She stepped into the elevator and took her phone out of her pocket. She read the message as the elevator travelled to the third floor. Just as the doors opened, she fumbled and dropped her phone, sending it plummeting towards the floor. But it didn't hit the floor. It fell perfectly into the gap between the elevator and the platform, down into what looked like a black hole.

"Oh, no!" she gasped. She felt guilty that her phone could actually be wedged into the mechanics of the elevator, potentially damaging it. She cringed as she confessed her mistake to the building's technician, who then had to work to retrieve the broken phone to stop it from damaging anything.

She was completely unfamiliar with the reception she was covering at, and the staff there looked at her with contempt throughout the day.

For the rest of the afternoon, she had to sit opposite the very elevator she had put out of commission. By 5pm, the elevator technician put the broken pieces of her phone in front of her.

She was never invited back.

Chapter Fifty-Two

****

It was close to the end of Melody's pregnancy. Her tummy had grown exceptionally large and she'd gained weight all over her body. It was a healthy amount of weight and didn't look excessive. Her face looked slightly fuller, but she still exuded a radiant glow and her skin was perfect. Melody's tummy truly did look like an orange at this stage. She ate healthy foods, full of fresh fruits and vegetables, and she felt strong. She experienced the normal aches and pains of a pregnant lady towards the end of her pregnancy, but she got through it without complaining. Besides, who would she complain to? The pillow on the couch?

It was becoming nearly impossible to put her shoes on in the morning. She had to set aside a good ten minutes to do so. It was winter, and her boots required lacing. Not ideal, really, for a lady about to give birth. But Melody didn't care. She was still enjoying her pregnancy. She went to pregnancy yoga, which taught her how to relax and feel the energy from Willow. Pregnancy yoga also taught her helpful techniques to use during labour, and her teacher passed on information about how to meditate, stay positive and be calm throughout the whole event. As well as going to yoga, Melody educated herself all about her impending labour by reading books on the subject. She didn't want anything to be a surprise on the day, so she worked hard to get an understanding of how her body would cope in labour. Melody truly believed that knowledge meant power. Power over herself; over hers and Willow's future. The education she'd committed herself to, helped her feel ready to welcome Willow into her world.

Melody joined some Freecycle websites local to London, close to the end of her pregnancy and collected absolutely everything she needed for Willow, free of charge. She struggled through Kentish Town with big bags of baby towels, clothes and bottles. It was no easy feat getting them home, on a freezing cold, rainy night, but she smiled as she walked with the bags. Her mood preceded her predicament. She knew that she was carrying the last set of bags to set her up in readiness for Willow's arrival, which would be soon. Very soon.

******

Melody passed her due date and became overdue. She ended up agreeing to have her labour induced and now everything she'd worked for, was impending. Her birth plan was written, she'd been to her ante-natal classes (the only single woman by herself again!) and her birth partners were at the ready. Her hospital bag sat packed by the front door. It seemed surreal and unbelievable to think the next time she walked through her front door, she would have a baby in her arms. Nervousness crept through her body. Could she go through labour and care for this little baby by herself? The self-doubt returned.

Her parents were staying in a hotel nearby. There was no room for them in her small apartment, which was full of baby things. She'd told them both how she managed to become pregnant, which didn't go down very well. It was over dinner at the hotel restaurant that she broke the news.

"There's something I would like to tell you, Mum and Dad."

They were finishing their dessert and stopped eating to look at her. They were both half-expecting this conversation.

"What's that?" asked her dad.

"I want to let you know how I became pregnant," Melody said.

"Well, I think we both know how that happened." Her mother laughed, rolling her eyes and looking at Melody's father.

"It's not how you think though," Melody said. She took a deep breath, then said, "I had IVF, via a donor."

Her parents looked at her in disbelief.

"That's what I was doing in New Zealand last time," Melody said.

"Why didn't you stay with us?" her mother asked. She was obviously annoyed and displeased with the unconventional nature of Melody's pregnancy.

"I wanted to relax at Indira's home to be close to the beach and play with her children to help me to prepare," Melody replied.

"Why couldn't I help you prepare?" her mother asked. She often got jealous when Melody chose to make big decisions in the company of others.

"I needed to relax, as I was taking a lot of

medication," Melody said.

"You could have relaxed with me," her mother said. "You could have stayed with us on the farm."

Melody sighed. "Thank you, Mum. It's just that sometimes we have, well, you know, disagreements."

"I really think you should have stayed with us," her mother replied.

"I didn't mean to be disrespectful. I just wanted to stay with Indira so I could relax," said Melody.

"Yeah, right," her father joined in. He, too, seemed angry.

"Let's go, Rhys. She doesn't need us," her mother said, standing up to leave. Her father put some money on the table.

Then, her parents walked towards the elevator to take them back to their room. This was not what Melody was expecting. She had hoped for their support. She really needed her parents right now. She needed their love and kindness. Melody followed her parents and caught up with them at the elevator.

"Please, you don't have to go. I need your support

right now. I didn't mean to disappoint you," she said frankly.

Her parents stepped into the elevator and pressed the number to the third floor. They didn't look at her and refused to say anything. The elevator doors slowly closed.

Melody, solemnly and slowly, walked back to her apartment. Only once she was safely back inside her apartment, did she cry heavy, sad tears. She felt alone. It was the first time ever that she'd asked for her parents' support, and they'd turned their backs on her. She placed protective arms around her belly and allowed her tears to slowly stop falling. Melody sat and rubbed her belly, and she felt her little girl move her legs around, getting more comfortable within her small space. Her breathing regained depth and she spoke softly to her bump.

"We can do this together, little Willow. We absolutely can. We have each other!" Melody said. "Willow and Mummy. Mummy and Willow."

Chapter Fifty-Three

****

It was late afternoon when Melody checked herself into hospital. She was taken straight to the maternity ward, where she joined five other ladies who had been induced or were about to be. There were six beds in total, each of which had its own curtain circled around the bed.

One woman, well into labour in the bed opposite Melody was trying desperately to regulate her breathing in-between shrieks of pain. Melody felt scared by the noises. It wasn't long before the maternity nurse wheeled her to the labour room for her to give birth. Her husband looked terrified and was holding her hand whilst she was in the wheelchair. It didn't look at all dignified. Melody hoped she would get through labour at least semi-gracefully, especially as her birth partners were her friends.

Grace walked into the ward and sat on a small chair next to Melody's bed, after giving her a reassuring hug. She was Melody's first birth partner. One by one, her other two birth partners arrived.

******

Francine was Melody's second birth partner. Melody met Francine just a couple of months after she'd arrived in London. Francine was French, and they both often wondered how they had become such good friends, because they simply couldn't understand each other back then. Melody had a strong New Zealander accent when she arrived all those years ago, and Francine was still getting a grasp of the English language. They were constantly repeating themselves. However, in time, Melody's accent mellowed, and Francine became more proficient in speaking English. Thereafter, their friendship blossomed. Francine had brunette hair, which was stylishly cut, was shorter than Melody and very petite. She was a man magnet and exuded vitality and vivaciousness. It was always a fun night whenever Francine was involved.

******

Rosita was Melody's last birth partner. She was going to help Melody through the most difficult part of her labour. Rosita was a Spanish lady with wavy shoulder-length black hair with red highlights and a voice that smiled. Melody met Rosita when they worked together on a service desk for a reputable blue chip company, and they were well-liked by the clients.

Whilst they worked, they constantly laughed and joked and genuinely enjoyed working together. One task they were given was checking which staff lockers were used or abandoned in the office. What they found in the old lockers made them laugh.

"Oh my goodness, Rosita, some of these lockers are so old, Napoleon himself had one!" Melody giggled.

Rosita laughed as she opened an old archived locker next to Melody jam-packed with discarded belongings. "Look, a letter to Napoleon from Josephine! Here's the wine they shared too!" Rosita joked, showing Melody some papers and an old can of Heineken. They laughed and laughed!

******

Now the three of them surrounded Melody on her hospital bed, joking about her current state of being.

"Hey, this induction business will be easy peasy," said Francine.

"Yeah, it will happen so quickly, you won't feel a thing!" injected Grace.

"Oh, I can feel her! Here she comes." Melody laughed, propping up her legs.

Rosita quickly ran to the bottom of the bed. "Ok, I'll catch her. Got her! One baby born, easy peasy!" Rosita chuckled as she pretended to catch a baby.

They all giggled and laughed, until by 10pm, the nurse suggested they were making too much noise and that visiting hours were now over. One by one, they gave Melody a hug and assured her they'd be in tomorrow.

Melody smiled well after they'd left. She was ready, but she was also happy to wait until the morning. She could try to sleep.

Then she felt a strange niggle in her belly. *Hhmmm, what was that? Could that be the beginning?* she thought.

It absolutely was. Her contractions had started. Very slowly and subtly, but they had begun.

Melody rang the buzzer by her bed. She asked one of the nurses to help her hook up her Tens machine. It just so happened the nurse had never seen a Tens machine before. Melody wasn't quite sure how that happened, as she thought they were mainstream, at least on the maternity forums she had read. She tried to stay calm as she read the instructions and directed the nurse where to place the pads for the machine on her back. It seemed quite complicated, but when she got the hang of how to use it, it helped a lot, as the pulse of the vibrations distracted her during her contractions.

Should Melody call Grace? No, it was okay, she'd be driving home, then going to bed. She'd be okay. She could do it! Between the Tens machine and Melody's ability to meditate during her contractions, she managed to get herself to nearly full dilation without assistance. To be honest, she'd expected the contractions to be much more painful. Melody managed her breathing and contractions so well that she was quiet all night. The meditation techniques she'd learnt at pregnancy yoga worked incredibly well for her. The nurses didn't realise how far gone she was until, eventually, Melody rang the buzzer in the morning. She summoned a nurse.

"I don't think I can handle this anymore. May I please have an epidural?" she asked. She remained calm and polite.

The nurse looked at her with amusement in her

eyes. "Let's take a look, shall we?" she said.

She examined Melody and panicked. "You're about to have this baby! It's way too late for an epidural. You've been so quiet!" she said, gasping and looking flustered.

"I thought it was going to be much worse!" Melody said. She was obviously in pain now. "But now it is!" Melody yelped.

The nurse rang the labour room to organise the midwife. She swiftly brought in a wheelchair for Melody. "Can you get in the wheelchair by yourself?" she asked.

"I don't think I can move!" said Melody.

The nurse helped her off the bed and into the wheelchair. She pushed Melody quickly, almost at running speed, to the labour room. Instantly, Melody was on another bed. In this room, she met the midwife, who introduced herself as Sophie. Sophie lifted Melody's hospital gown.

"You're going to have this baby very soon. Do you have anyone to support you?" Sophie asked.

"Yes, but I haven't called them. I thought I had ages to go yet!" Melody replied, before inhaling deeply the gas that was now available to her.

Sophie used Melody's phone under her instruction to text Grace. Melody didn't think she'd make it on time. She couldn't think about it. All she could think about was pushing her baby out. She needed to push her out, immediately. She opted for leaning forward on a birthing ball to push. She leaned on it and tried her hardest, but the pushing was incredibly difficult! To her surprise, Grace arrived in no time.

"Here I am," she said. "Oh, Melody! It's happening!"

"Melody, I'm going to burst your waters," Sophie said.

"Okay," was all Melody could say.

Sophie informed her, "Your baby has done her first poo inside you; you've got to get her out now, and you only have thirty minutes to do so."

Pressuuurreee, Melody thought.

Grace encouraged her, giving her sips of water and jelly beans as she kept trying to push.

"Fifteen minutes left," said Sophie.

"Ten minutes left," she said.

"You've only got five minutes left," Sophie informed her.

"I'm trying," Melody said. She was sweating and her hair was plastered to her face, but she never once screamed or yelled. Her voice remained at a low level and she still remained polite and calm throughout the birth.

"It's been thirty minutes," said Sophie. She rang the doctor and the paediatrician, who were in the room within seconds. Melody was helped onto the bed as it was briskly transformed. Half of the bed broke away, and stirrups were folded out.

The doctor, who was a woman, asked, "Can I cut you a little, Melody?"

"Just do whatever you have to, Doctor," Melody said, exhaling louder than she spoke.

Melody was injected with pain relief at the site and the doctor made the incision. After a slight uncomfortable prick of the needle, she felt nothing.

"Right, on your next contraction, Melody, you need to push as hard as you can," the doctor told her.

Melody felt the next contraction wave and she summoned all her energy to push. She pushed as hard as she could.

"Well done, Melody, your baby's head is out!" the doctor said. "Next contraction, another big push." The doctor was calm and professional, reassuring Melody. Grace held her hand tightly.

On the next wave, Melody gave an almighty push. She thought the lower half of her body was about to come apart! Then she felt like a part of her had been sucked out. It was surreal.

"You did it, Melody. You did it!" everyone cried out.

She felt as though she was going to faint. She strained her ears to hear any sounds from her little girl. Suddenly, she panicked. There was no sound.

Melody's baby was put on a table, and the paediatrician leant over her and helped her to clear her lungs. Then the clearest baby cry radiated throughout the room.

"A beautiful, healthy, gorgeous little baby girl," said the midwife, placing her on Melody.

"We did it, Willow! We did it together!" Melody cried. She was weeping as she looked at her baby daughter, consumed by elation, happiness and relief.

"Hello, Willow," Melody gently said to her daughter, kissing her forehead. Her lovely little girl opened her eyes and looked at her mummy. Her skin was warm against Melody's and her cheeks were a rose pink colour. Melody looked into Willow's eyes and smiled deeply. She thought she saw Willow smiling back.

Just then, Rosita came running into the room. "I'm here, I'm here! Did I miss anything?" she cried.

Chapter Fifty-Four

****

Melody left Willow in the care of Grace, whilst Rosita helped her walk to the shower room. After Melody assured Rosita that she was now steady on her feet and could be left alone, she slowly undressed. It was very strange seeing her now saggy and very wobbly belly, with no child in there to keep her skin taut. Strangely, she hadn't been expecting that. Her mind had been entirely focused on her baby. Melody enjoyed the hot water on her face and she washed away her perspiration.

We did it, she thought to herself. *I did it! I gave birth and we both survived!*

She relished the relief she felt. Everything had gone well and that her little girl was healthy. Melody stood in the shower room and enjoyed the warmth on her body. As soon as she closed her eyes, she immediately saw Dexter.

He was young and healthy, now. Fun times they'd

shared together flooded her consciousness. Visions of them dancing together, holding hands, kissing, laughing, sharing birthdays, moving in together, cuddling each other on top of the Peak in Hong Kong, hiking in Cambodia, and standing at the top of the London Eye, feeling like they were about to take on the world.

Melody clenched her hands together and placed them under her chin. Then, she looked up towards the ceiling and sent out a message to Dexter.

"Thank you," she whispered.

Chapter Fifty-Five

****

Melody and Willow were surrounded by visitors that afternoon. Her parents arrived after everyone had left as well. They were proud of their granddaughter, and Melody could tell that this little girl would bring their family together. How amazing that such a tiny little bundle can do something so wonderful, simply by existing.

When everybody had finally left, Melody cradled Willow and softly stroked her forehead. This little girl was so special and gorgeous. She looked peaceful being cuddled in her mummy's arms. Melody took Willow's tiny feet in her hands and counted her toes. Ten lovely toes. Melody smiled, then held Willow's tiny hands and gently rubbed her fingers. Two thumbs and eight lovely long fingers. They were perfectly formed. Melody felt proud.

What an adventure it had been to finally have this precious little girl today. Melody had fallen in love, taken a chance, had her heart broken and made sacrifices. She'd grown so much through the journey, which she'd been brave enough to take on by herself.

As Melody sat holding Willow close to her chest, she daydreamed... She saw Willow as a primary school child, growing up, running through the wheat fields at her parents' farm. She saw Willow going to school, blossoming, even getting married and having children of her own one day. Melody was going to be there to help and support her in any way she could.

She held her daughter close to her heart, then whispered softly, "Love can conquer all."

REVIEW REQUEST

If you loved reading this story

As much as I did too

Please write a review and submit

For everyone online to view

Love Kayla xx

(I am a Self Published Author and reviews are important for me to be successful. I would be very thankful if you could find the time to send in a review with your honest feedback.)

LOOK OUT FOR MY NEXT BOOK

"Wishing For An Angel"

YOU CAN FIND ME AT...

kaylacmcintyre.com

kaylacmcintyre@gmail.com

https://twitter.com/kaylacmcintyre

https://www.facebook.com/kaylacmcintyre.author

www.ingramcontent.com/pod-product-compliance
Lightning Source LLC
LaVergne TN
LVHW041631060526
838200LV00040B/1527